The Red Priest's Annina

Sarah Bruce Kelly

Bel Canto Press

www.belcantopress.com

ISBN 978-0-578-02566-7

Cover Art: Porträt von Molly und Peggy mit Zeichenutensilien
(Thomas Gainsborough, 1760)

For Annina, who speaks to me through her music, and who has inspired me to sing her song.

CHAPTER 1

Il Prete Rosso

The Red Priest

Mantua, Northern Italy 1721

I bit back the song I ached to sing. Papà didn't allow it. He said it was unseemly for a girl to flaunt herself like that in public. What would his customers think? Besides, it distracted him from his work.

My father and I were in his wig shop. I was counting coins while he worked at his account books. The task was monotonous but better than the tedious stitchery I'd left behind at our cheerless house, scattered and neglected. Helping Papà in his shop was my escape from that wearisome chore.

But I was still fidgety. My eyes scanned the dozens of

goat hair and human hair wigs Papà had carefully crafted, perched on wooden blockheads and displayed along shelves that lined the wall behind the counter where I sat. The blockheads' blank faces looked as bored as I felt. I closed my eyes for a moment and breathed in the comforting scents of lavender and orange flower drifting from the cans of hair powder Papà kept under the counter. The aromas reminded me of Mamma.

I placed the last silver ducat in the coin box and recorded the amount. Then I rested my chin in my hand and drummed my fingers to the beat of a tune playing in my head, the melody of an aria Mamma used to sing with me. Soon the melody found its way to my throat and became a hum, and my fingers drummed faster:

Humming, drumming, humming, drumming.

My voice yearned to break free, and I sprang to my feet as an explosion of song surged through me. Even Papà's groaning and head-shaking couldn't break the spell I was under. My outstretched arms trembled with a misty yearning as I sang, *My heart beats faster when I see your sparkling eyes—*

The bell over the shop door clanged, and the October wind heralded the entrance of a dapper looking young gentleman. I gasped, and my cheeks flamed with embarrassment.

The man's grin exuded charm. "*Brava*, signorina," he said, clapping his hands. "That was splendid. What emotion, what sincerity of feeling. We could use more like you in the opera."

I felt the blood rushing through my veins, but for Papà's sake I tried to harness my excitement. I dipped my chin modestly and dropped a curtsy.

The gentleman held his tri-cornered hat to his chest and greeted my father with a polite nod.

Papà's bow was fawning. "Your Excellency, what an honor it is, as always, that you grace my humble shop with your noble presence." Then he glanced at me and frowned. "You must excuse my naughty Annina's improper behavior, Excellency. I simply do not know what to do with her. She refuses to sit still and attend to her duties like a proper, well-behaved young lady of her station."

"There's nothing to excuse, Signor Girò," the man said, smiling. "Your charming daughter should be on the stage. She's quite an actress."

Papà's expression was a combination of horror and simpering reproach. "You are too kind, Excellency, but naturally I could never permit my daughter to perform in a theater."

Still smiling, the man turned to me and winked. "Perhaps we can change his mind, Signorina Annina."

I nodded eagerly.

He turned back to my father. "I regret, signore, that I'm here to cancel my wig order and to bring you unpleasant news. The empress in Vienna has died, and a period of mourning has been ordered throughout the Austrian Empire. All the theaters in the monarchy will close immediately. Don Antonio Vivaldi has just resigned his position at the court of Mantua and will return to Venice straightaway, along with his entire entourage."

My heart leaped with rapture at the mention of Don Antonio, then sank with sorrow at the news of his departure.

"He'll resume his teaching post at the *conservatorio* of the Pietà," the man said, "and he already has plans to begin rehearsing his newest opera at the Teatro San Angelo, *La verità in cimento*, in which my protégée, Chiara Orlandi, will sing a starring role. Thus I must bid *addio* to your fair city and return to my Venetian home."

"This is most distressing news," my father said.

I knew his distress wasn't about the opera closing down. The enforced period of mourning would also close down his wig shop.

"Please accept this trifle for your trouble, signore," the gentleman said, handing my father a sizable coin.

Papà bowed his appreciation as the man put on his hat, winked at me again, and left the shop.

"Papà, who was that man?" I asked.

"That was the Duke of Massa Carrara, a fine gentleman and a great patron of the opera."

"I don't understand, Papà. Why does our opera theater have to close just because an empress died in Vienna?"

"Mantua is a southern province of the Habsburg monarchy, Annina *mia.* Therefore it's part of the Austrian Empire, as is much of Italy. So we must abide by their laws."

"Why don't the theaters in Venice have to close?"

"Venice isn't under Habsburg rule. It's an independent republic. There is no city like it in the world."

Excitement swept through me. "Can't we move there, Papà?"

He looked horrified. "Certainly not. Venice is a city of vice, and the people there care for nothing but merriment. Look how it corrupted your mother."

Mamma had always been moody and distant, but I still missed her terribly. She and Papà argued a lot, and she'd left home several months before, after a blaring fight. None of us knew where she'd gone. Since then my much older half-sister, Paolina, had taken over the household duties. I helped her as much as I could, but my grief over Mamma's absence didn't leave me much energy for chores. Secretly, I was afraid my unruly nature had been the real reason Mamma left. A dark, nagging fear told me Papà and Paolina might reject me for the same reason.

To cheer me up, Papà sometimes let me go with him to the royal theater when he delivered wigs and hairpieces for the opera performances. I loved to watch our visiting musical celebrity, who I called Don Antonio, rehearse the singers and orchestra. Others called him *il Prete Rosso* because he was a priest-musician, and because of the color of his hair.

The first time I saw him he was practicing with the other musicians. I was transfixed. His fingers flew like lightning over his violin strings, and his music sparkled with fire, as did his golden red hair and deep blue eyes.

One day I boldly approached him during a rehearsal break. I told him how my mother and I used to sing opera arias together and that *his* were my favorites. He listened kindly, and his interest seemed so heartfelt. His smile made me tingle.

From that moment his music filled my mind, and his name echoed in my heart. But now that he was leaving Mantua I felt again like I was sinking in darkness.

ONE FRIGID EVENING in mid January I sat at the little spinet in our parlor, trying to pick out the melody of an aria Mamma used to sing with me. As usual my needlework was spread across the nearby worktable, gathering dust. I glanced at Papà. He sat by the hearth and gazed into the spitting flames. To my surprise he motioned me to his side.

I scurried to him and knelt at his knee. "What is it,

Papà?"

"My dearest Annina, this breaks my heart, but I must send you away." His eyes were moist, and my belly curled into a knot.

"Send me away? What do you mean, Papà?"

"Our noble friend, His Excellency, the Duke of Massa Carrara, has written me. He has generously offered to sponsor your tuition to study music in Venice, so it seems you will get your wish."

My insides swirled with a mixture of thrill and alarm. "Will you go with me?" I asked, breathless.

"No, my love, I can't go with you. Paolina will accompany you on the journey and see that you arrive safely. Like your mother, she grew up in Venice and knows the city well."

"You mean . . . she'll leave me there all alone?"

"Not alone, little one. His Excellency has arranged for you to lodge at the house of Signora Malvolia Berardi, a former opera singer but a respectable lady all the same. I believe His Excellency's protégée, Signorina Chiara, resides there as well. Chiara is from a good family here in Mantua, the Orlandis. So I'm confident you'll be safe and secure in Venice, among friends, which will be a great comfort to me."

"But I feel safe here with you and Paolina," I said, clutching his knees.

"You must trust me that this is for the best, my Annina.

The duke's offer is a rare opportunity. To turn him down would be an insult."

Panic whisked through me, and tears pricked my eyes. I laid my head on his knee. "I don't want to go, Papà. I don't want to leave you."

He stroked my hair. "Your mother's gone, and my business is failing. Your poor sister is carrying the burden for all of us, and I worry that it'll become too much for her. It will help us to know you're well cared for. And with the education and refinement you will acquire under Signora Malvolia's guardianship, you'll attract a suitable husband."

"But I don't want a husband, Papà, I want to sing in the opera," I whimpered, my tears splotching the soft wool of his knee breeches.

He sighed wearily. "Be a good girl and do as I say, Annina *mia*."

There was no point arguing with him. Blinking back my tears, I looked up at him and wiped my nose with the back of my hand. "When will I go?"

"Next week. Paolina will help you prepare."

I was fourteen but felt as helpless as a frightened little girl, aching to be picked up and cuddled.

CHAPTER 2

La Moretta

The Black Mask

I gazed across the blue expanse of water that surrounds Mantua. The town's arches and spires faded into the background as our small sailing vessel approached the Mincio River, on its journey east to the Adriatic Sea. Papà had told me the duke would arrange for me to study singing with Don Antonio, and my eagerness to see him again overshadowed my anxiety about living away from home.

The next day, salty sea air and the shrill of gulls flooded my senses when we sailed into the Adriatic and veered north. By the time our little ship made its way into the Venetian lagoon a pearly haze was spreading across the clear blue sky, signaling the approach of sunset. In the dimming light I smelled the crystal scent of winter in the air and tasted its iciness on my tongue. Clenching my cloak about myself, I gaped in awe at the towers and domes of Venice, aglow in the pink and orange hues of twilight like an enchanted city that had risen out of the water's murky depths.

The lagoon was crowded with sea craft of all kinds, and it seemed our boat would never reach the harbor. In fact, we had come to a standstill. Paolina and I gazed over the rail. An unusual looking rowing vessel glided beneath us, and a leather-faced man smiled up at us with a yellowed, gap-toothed grin. He lifted his brimless red cap.

Paolina leaned toward me and cupped her hand around her mouth. "That's a gondola, the main form of transportation around Venice."

"I'll get you lovely ladies into town faster than this rickety excuse for a sea vessel ever will," the cheery gondolier called to us in *veneziano*, the colorful language peculiar to Venice.

The city's obscure dialect wasn't a problem for me, thanks to my Venetian mother and sister.

Paolina frowned down at the gondolier. "What is your fee, sir?"

His price was high, but he quickly added that for such charming *donzelle* he was willing to make an exception.

"I've heard about swindlers like you," Paolina said.

"So de chi che te parla," the man said, with a pained expression and hand on his heart, "I know what you're talk-

ing about. But I assure you, signora, my price is the best you'll find."

Paolina kept frowning but finally agreed to the *gondoliere*'s offer. He handed each of us down the ladder that descended into his gondola, along with my small trunk and the rest of our meager baggage. We settled into a cushioned seat, and the gondola smoothly slid away from the boat.

My eyes drank in the panorama of enticing sights. Houses and other buildings seemed magically built on the water's surface. There were no coaches or horses, only boats of all shapes and sizes.

The gondolier studied us curiously. "What brings such fine ladies as you to Venice?"

Paolina gave my wrist a warning squeeze. "My sister is here to study music."

"Is that so?" The boatman's rough face brightened with interest. "And what instrument do you play, young miss?"

I was too excited to hold my tongue. "I'm going to study singing, and someday I'll sing in the opera."

Paolina's mouth hardened into a thin line.

The gondolier laughed into the brisk evening air. "Well, you've sure come to the right place, miss. We Venetians are so smitten with the opera our theaters are packed to the rafters every night. I'll be there myself this evening."

"You will?" I was fascinated such a coarse character would be so interested in the opera.

"I will indeed. We *gondolieri* are the greatest admirers, and the sharpest critics I daresay, of opera singing. The theater managers prize our support so much they give us free tickets." He drew himself up proudly. "They know we'll tout our favorite singers to the rich foreigners who pack Venice during the opera season. That means more business, and more profit, for the operatic bigwigs." His leathery face stretched into a knowing grin as he swept the heavy oar through glistening water.

My whole body prickled with excitement. "What opera will you see tonight, sir?"

"Well, miss, there're so many choices. At least six different shows going on this evening, I hear. But I'm itching to go to the Teatro San Angelo. That's where my favorite composer, *il Prete Rosso,* puts on most of his operas."

I almost sprang from my seat.

"But tonight Maestro Tomaso Albinoni's opening his new opera there. Sad to say, *il Prete Rosso* isn't putting on an opera here this season. Not sure why. Too busy teaching and composing, I s'pose. Who knows, miss, you may well be studying with him soon. Before we know it, *you'll* be up there onstage singing in one of his operas."

My heart beat with so much violence I thought it would jump out of my chest. "Paolina, can't we please,

please go to the opera tonight?"

She sighed and looked heavenward.

I turned pleading eyes to our friendly gondolier. "Won't you help me convince her, sir?"

"Hush, Annina," Paolina said. "I think you've annoyed this gentleman quite enough with your silly chatter."

"She's not bothering me, ma'am," he said, smiling. "I like to see a girl with a *temperamento brioso*."

At last, someone who appreciated my spirited temperament. Venice's allure was growing by the minute.

The gondola's fender brushed a concrete platform, and I felt a slight jolt. A dock worker secured the boat to a post with heavy rope, and our gallant boatman bounded off his perch and helped us step up to the *fondamenta*, pavement. "*Piazza San Marco*," he said, with a sweeping gesture. "Welcome to *Carnevale!*"

There could be nothing else in the world so filled with glittering surprise as the scene I beheld. A massive cathedral loomed over the swarms of merry-makers who crammed the square, their faces shrouded in lurid masks. Countless lanterns and torches bathed the sprawling spectacle in brilliant light.

My jaw dropped as an explosion of colors filled the sky.

"*Fuochi d'artificio*," the gondolier said as he lifted my trunk to the *fondamenta*. I turned to him, and an artless grin spread across his face. "I wager you'll be lighting up the stage with your own fireworks before we know it, miss." He lifted his cap and hopped back in the boat.

Paolina called after him, "Excuse me, sir—" But he'd already rowed out of hearing, no doubt anxious to drum up more business before the opera. "*Santo cielo*, holy heavens. I was going to ask him for directions to the house where the duke's arranged for us to stay tonight." She sighed heavily. "Oh well, maybe someone can direct us."

Baggage in tow, we made our way toward the motley throng that crowded the *piazza*. Soon we were caught in a whirl of masked revelers. Clowns and harlequins capered about, and jugglers and acrobats displayed their marvels. Fiddles sang, guitars murmured, feet pattered, and voices hummed. The pleasant noise and sea-scented air weren't spoiled by the clatter of horse hooves and wheels, and reek of manure that bombard the senses in other cities.

I stared in wonder at faceless figures in ghostly white masks topped with black tri-cornered hats and wrapped in long, dark cloaks. Others wore sparkly masks, and many were dressed in exotic costumes. I was so caught up in the jumble of images and sensations that I bumped headlong into a dusky-eyed woman dressed in filmy turquoise, as the scent of spicy perfume filled my nostrils.

Her eyes narrowed and glowered at me over the glimmering veil that hid the lower half of her face. "*You will suffer much*." The woman's hissing tone and strange accent sharpened the sting of her sinister words.

My heart lurched. "*Scusi*—" I fumbled to apologize, but she cut me off.

"*La moretta.* She will shelter you."

I gawked dumbly at the ghoulish black mask she'd shoved into my hand, unsure how such an evil looking thing could protect me.

"*La moretta* was given to me by a countess, as payment for telling her fortune," the woman said. "She has much value. But for you, one *soldo*."

I scrambled through my satchel for one of the few small coins Papà had tearfully pressed into my palm as we said our goodbyes.

Paolina tugged my arm. "*Annina*."

But I was lost in the mysterious lady's mesmerizing gaze. With shaking fingers I pulled a coin from my satchel and handed it to her.

She took it eagerly as her eyes bore into mine. "There are no bands or strings. Inside the mask there is *un bottone*, a button you will clutch with your teeth. You will have no voice. The silence of *la moretta* will shield you."

Before I could think what to say, she was swept back into the crowd and out of sight.

My sister's face was pinched with anger. "How could you, Annina? How could you throw away Papà's hard-earned money on that piece of rubbish?"

"Didn't you hear what the lady said, Paolina? She's a *chiromante*, a fortune-teller. She must be very wise."

"What a pack of nonsense. She's a thieving Gypsy if I ever saw one. I honestly don't know what's to become of you, Annina. You haven't got a grain of common sense in your head."

A shiver of fear swept through me—not at my sister's scolding words, but at what the woman had said: *You will suffer much.*

Groaning, Paolina shook her head and continued pushing her way through the crowd, with me close at her heels. We passed through one of the arcades that enclose the *piazza* and found ourselves surrounded by a baffling complex of narrow canals and *calli*, cramped alleyways.

At a shadowy canal junction we gasped in unison as two passenger-less gondolas collided. We gawked speechlessly at the storm of insults that followed.

"*Baùko!*" shrieked one gondolier, in vivid *veneziano*, "you idiot! You've wrecked my boat!"

"*Ti xe goldon!*" the other one shouted back, "you ass! It was my right to enter the canal first!"

Fury mounted, and they reviled each other as the offspring of assassins and prostitutes.

"Spawn of a bloody executioner!"

"Bastard of a hideous whore!"

Fists waved and hammered palms, and faces contorted. With a vehemence that would make the devil blush, they each defamed the other's female relatives down to the remotest cousin. Finally, his passion spent, one of the men gathered his oar and gave the other the right of way.

"What ruffians," my sister said, after the two gondoliers had peacefully departed. "I would've asked them for directions, but I feared for our lives."

I was more fascinated than afraid. "That's the most exciting thing I've ever seen!"

"*Santo cielo*, Annina, sometimes I have to wonder about your sense of propriety." Exasperated, Paolina fished through her satchel and drew out a folded leaf of paper. She opened it and squinted in the candlelight that illumined a street-corner shrine to the Blessed Virgin. "Oh, I don't know." She sighed and glanced around. "Let's try this direction."

The streets of Venice, laced with the city's continuous web of canals, were like catacombs in their dark narrowness and obscurity. The constant sound of water slapping the hulls of gondolas echoed from every wall and resounded eerily through every tunnel and passageway. I slung my satchel over my shoulder and clung to Paolina's arm, while I gazed about at the bewildering maze of concrete and stucco that entombed the mysterious *calli*.

Finally we came to what seemed to be a theater district. I looked up and a sharp thrill flickered through me. The playbill outside a *teatro* we were passing announced the premier of Tomaso Albinoni's opera *L'Eccissi della Gelosia.* A man in a red cloak strutted up and down in front of the theater hawking tickets.

I tightened my grip on my sister's arm. "Paolina! Here's the Teatro San Angelo. This is where the gondolier said Don Antonio puts on most of his operas. And look, the sign tells about the opera that's opening tonight. I think it's the one he was telling us about. Look at the opera's name, The Excesses of Jealousy. Doesn't that sound exciting? And we can buy the tickets right here. Oh, please, Paolina, *per piacere*."

"I can't imagine anything more foolish, Annina. Papà would be incensed at the idea. Even if you were allowed to go we can't afford it, especially after you squandered good money on that worthless Carnival mask. You know perfectly well that with the setbacks Papà's had, his business isn't going well. Anyway, this isn't even Don Antonio's opera."

Tears stung my eyes. "But Paolina, you don't know how important this is to me."

"Annina, stop this at once. We're going to find Signora Roselli's guest house. She's expecting us, and it would be rude to keep her waiting. And my back aches from lugging this trunk. I don't plan to do anything tonight except have a little supper and a bath, and go to bed."

My lip started to tremble.

Paolina's eyes softened, and the hard corners of her mouth relaxed. "Now Annina, this is no way to start your new life in Venice. I don't want you to spend our last evening together upset." She smoothed a strand of wispy brown hair from my forehead and sighed. "All right, then. Let's see how much the tickets are."

My cheeks stretched into a grin, and I threw my arms around her neck.

"Are you trying to strangle me?" she said, reaching to unfasten my clasping arms. "Now listen to me. You must promise not to say one word about this to your father. He'd never forgive me. And you must promise to stay by my side every minute."

"Yes, yes, yes," I said, hardly able to keep from jumping up and down. "I'll be so good you won't even know me." I grasped my sister's hand and pulled her toward the red-cloaked man.

After several inquiries we came across a boy bearing a lantern who presented himself as a "city guide." For a small fee he led us through a maze of bleak pathways to Signora Roselli's house. She greeted us warmly and led us to a modest bedchamber. We freshened up and enjoyed a savory supper of pasta, tomatoes, and crispy fried minnows before we set out for the opera.

INSIDE THE *TEATRO*, the riot of vibrant colors and sparkling lights was *una festa*, a feast for my eyes. Elaborate crystal chandeliers hung from the ceiling and held hundreds of twinkling candles. Four tiers of red-painted, gold-gilded opera boxes, filled with chattering, laughing people, lined the walls of the cozy theater and both sides of the stage. I was glad, though, that we'd bought the cheaper tickets and were on the ground level, called the "pit."

Paolina and I found seats on a wooden bench just behind the orchestra, barely managing to cram ourselves among the rowdy opera fans. Hawkers roamed the pit offering candied fruits and nuts for two *soldi*, with the toothpick they were skewered on thrown into the bargain. I glanced around, hoping to catch a glimpse of our gondolier. But the noisy mob that crowded the pit made it impossible to see past the second row.

Musicians started to wander in and take their seats. They spread out their music scores and tuned their instruments. A scowling, hump-shouldered man shuffled toward the harpsichord, a thick score under his arm. White bristles jutted from his sagging jowls, and stringy gray hair hung straight and limp from his balding head. He sat at the harpsichord, placed the score on the rack, and tugged at his coattails.

That must be Maestro Tomaso, I thought, with a dim feeling of disgust.

After the opening *sinfonia*, the orchestral introduction, the curtain rose and a man and woman in exotic costumes sang a melodic dialogue, known as *recitative*. The two characters were having a lovers' quarrel, and the force of their verbal combat made my insides quiver. I fidgeted with excitement when the male character broke into a rousing aria about his jealousy over his lover's infidelity. At one point a dazzling fountain of notes gushed from his mouth, and I couldn't control my restlessness another minute. I leaped from my seat and darted to the edge of the orchestra area, clutched the railing, and strained on tiptoe to get a closer view of the singer.

"*Annina*." My sister's voice was a harsh whisper as she grasped my arm. "Stay in your seat or we are leaving this theater."

I looked about at people eating, drinking, playing cards, and socializing in the dozens of opera boxes that surrounded us. "But other people are moving around and talking."

"That's their business. You said you wanted to see the opera, and I expect you to behave like a lady."

I went back to my seat and tried hard to sit still. But as the drama unfolded my excitement grew. Maestro Tomaso's opera didn't have the energy and liveliness of Don Antonio's music, but the singers' expressive performances thrilled me just the same. My eyes stayed riveted to the stage until the opera's finale, when everyone's differences were resolved and a chorus sang of the sunny skies that shine forth after dark clouds and storms have passed. I watched the curtain fall on the final act and knew this was what I wanted to do with my life.

"Don Antonio's going to teach me to sing like that, and I'll star in his operas one day," I said as we stepped into the cold night air.

Paolina frowned. "Don't be such a goose and start getting yourself worked up for nothing," she said, brushing a lock of hair from my eye. "Don Antonio is one of the most famous composers in all of Europe and the most sought-after music teacher in Venice. Do you really think he has the patience to put up with a silly nymph like you?"

"But Paolina—"

"Seriously, Annina, you'll save yourself a lot of trouble and heartache if you learn to be more practical. I can't bear to think of you bringing senseless misery on yourself chasing some wild fantasy. You're here in Venice to study the ladylike art of music until the time is right for Papà to find you a proper husband. So you must learn to harness these reckless passions of yours and become more realistic. I only say this for your own good, because I want you to be happy."

My spirits slumped. She had no idea what would make me happy. No one did.

CHAPTER 3

La Lezione di Canto

The Singing Lesson

My stomach was aflutter with dread at the thought of saying goodbye to Paolina. I hugged myself and watched her whisk a tear from the corner of her eye, while our gondola glided along Venice's Canale Grande through the frigid morning fog.

My growing agitation forced me to speak up. "Paolina, why can't you stay with me at Signora Malvolia's?"

She gazed at me with sad eyes. "You know that's not possible, Annina. I must get home to Papà. He can't manage alone just now."

I thought about this. "You're more loyal to Papà than any of us. But he's not even your real father."

"He's been a father to me for most of my life. Lord

only knows what would have happened to Mamma and me after my own father died, if it hadn't been for him."

"Did Mamma love Papà then?" I asked in a small voice.

Paolina didn't answer right away.

"Marrying him was better than the alternatives," she finally said.

"What do you mean?"

"I mean a woman can't get by without a male protector, unless she wants to end up in a convent—or a brothel."

I shuddered. "Couldn't Mamma have followed her dream of singing in the opera?"

She gave me a stern look. "The theater is no better than a brothel, Annina. It's time you learned that."

I sighed and shifted in my seat.

"I can't abandon Papà now, like Mamma has done," Paolina said softly, with a slight tremor in her voice.

And what about me? Mamma abandoned me too.

The thrill that swelled in me blotted out every trace of self-pity. Soon, maybe even today, I would begin my studies with Don Antonio. My heart sang with happiness.

Our gondola entered the broad waters of the Canale di San Marco, and the hazy outlines of the many buildings that line Venice's rippling waterways came to life as slivers of candlelight poured from countless windows and gilded the early morning mist. A gleaming, whitewashed structure on my right towered above its surroundings, a cross rising from its gabled roof.

"*Santa Maria della Pietà*," our gondolier announced.

The girls' foundling home and conservatory where Don Antonio teaches music, I thought, as I quivered with almost unbearable bliss.

A moment later the gondolier docked and lifted my trunk onto the *fondamenta.* The boardinghouse where the duke had arranged for me to stay was across a short footbridge from the Pietà. It was comforting to know Don Antonio would be so near.

Paolina sounded the bell at the house's main entrance, which overlooked the San Marco Canal. A young girl in a maid's cap and apron ushered us inside, then led the gondolier down a dark hall, my trunk on his shoulder.

An old lady stood in the foyer, dressed entirely in black. Her withering stare made my throat clench. I felt gagged.

"I am Signora Malvolia, proprietress of this boardinghouse," she said. "I understand you are here in Venice to study music, under the patronage of the Duke of Massa Carrara."

The air, thick with the stench and taste of mildew, was dizzying.

"*Sì*," I said, as I sank into a curtsy with legs as wobbly as a newborn colt's.

She pursed her lips and looked me over. "They call

you Annina?"

I nodded warily.

"You may call me Signora,"she said, her lips tightening.

"*Sì*, Signora."

"And you are fourteen years of age?"

"*Sì*, Signora."

"You're beginning your studies rather late, aren't you?"

Signora's smirking gaze left me speechless. Despair slithered through me like a viper.

"You will begin your lessons this afternoon, with Maestro Tomaso," she said.

I remembered the surly looking maestro I'd seen at the opera the night before, and my creeping despair turned to panic. I wanted to scream. All that came out was a strangled whisper. "The duke said I would study with Don Antonio."

"Don Antonio has left Venice," she said, her tone as dry as the clumps of dust that hovered in the foyer's shadowy corners.

My heart wavered, then plunged with a sickening clunk.

"Where is he?" I managed to ask.

"He is in Rome."

"But why did he leave Venice?"

"It is not your place to ask questions." Her icy glare shriveled my insides.

My eyes darted frantically about the gloomy foyer. January's bleakness seemed to have seeped through its walls along with the dank smell of rotting stone.

"I'd like to speak to the duke about this," I finally said, lifting my chin. I tried to sound bold but couldn't stop my lip from quivering.

The corners of Signora's mouth twisted into a stuffy sort of smile. "His Excellency has left town on business and will be away for some time. He's prepaid your room and board here as well as your tuition with Maestro Tomaso. And now it is time to bid your sister farewell so my maid, Bettina, can show you to your chamber."

Paolina lingered by the front door. I ran to her and threw my arms around her neck. The faint scent of lavender, which reminded me so much of Mamma, turned my eyes to liquid. She held me close.

"We don't tolerate displays of emotion here," Signora said, gripping my shoulders and pulling me from my sister's arms.

Through clouded eyes I caught a glimpse of Paolina's worried face before she kissed my forehead and said, "Goodbye, Annina. Write to me." She turned and gave me one last glance as Bettina ushered her out.

Pain jabbed my belly as I wondered how long it would be before I'd see my sister or parents again.

I followed Bettina down the gloomy hall that led to the stairs. Along the way, she pointed out a closet-like room containing a dusty, ancient looking keyboard instrument. "That's where the singers here do their practicing, miss," she said. "Signora will assign you a daily practice time. Yours will probably be early in the morning since all the other times are taken."

Further down the hall, toward the kitchen, we passed another open door. I peered into a cramped room and saw a plump young woman, busy with needlework. She looked up at me and smiled, her eyebrows arched with curiosity, then jutted out her lower lip and blew upwards to doff a lock of straw-colored hair from her eye. Her hands never left her sewing.

I felt a brief flicker of warmth. The seamstress's cozy smile was a fleeting comfort.

Bettina led me up a dark, enclosed stairway to a tiny bedchamber. The room's scant furniture consisted of a cot, a mirror-less washstand, and a flimsy looking wardrobe cabinet. I squinted at the morning sunlight that peeked through a narrow window overlooking the San Marco Canal.

"The necessary's at the end of the hall, miss, last door on the left," Bettina said before disappearing down the stairwell.

I dreaded having to grope my way down that spooky corridor in the dead of night, should I need to relieve myself.

Alone in my room, I opened my trunk and took out

the two extra dresses I'd brought, smoothed them, and hung them in the wardrobe. I draped my dressing gown on a hook attached to the door. Since there was no chest of drawers, I dragged my trunk to the foot of the cot to store my nightgowns, underclothes, and my few other belongings.

I emptied my satchel onto the bed, and my eyes met *la moretta*'s dark stare. Pushing the rest of my odds and ends to the side, I picked up the mask and looked it over carefully in the morning sunlight. "She" was molded from stiff leather and shrouded in black velvet. I held her to my face. She felt cold and hard, stifling. Slowly my teeth grasped the little wooden *bottone*, meant to both silence and protect a girl. I quickly pulled *la moretta* from my face and slipped her into the trunk.

Then I lay down, wrapped my arms around myself, stared at the ceiling, and tried not to cry. My heart, which only a few minutes ago had bubbled over with such happy anticipation, was now drained of hope. I felt trapped, and utterly alone.

AT THE MIDDAY MEAL I met three of the other singers who lodged at Signora's house. They all looked a little older than I was, and I soon learned they'd been students of Maestro Tomaso for several years.

Ernesta, the quietest of the group, seemed to make a point of avoiding my eyes. With raised chin, she set her mouth in a priggish little frown. Then there was Marzia, who continually cut her eyes to me and just as quickly looked away, giving me the uneasy feeling I was being watched. The oldest looking of the trio was Fiametta. Her face was dominated by a hawk-like nose and toothy smile, and she almost never stopped talking.

I sat in troubled silence and moved my food around with my fork. Bettina had served steaming plates of boiled beef and vegetables, but I felt like there was a lightning storm in my stomach. I couldn't swallow a bite. The grating sound of Fiametta's constant chatter only aggravated my distress. When she finally paused to take a breath, I turned to Signora and asked if anyone else lived at her house.

Before she could answer, Fiametta interrupted with her booming voice. "Well of course there's our resident *celebrity*—our very own singing star."

I glanced around the table and noticed the other two girls respond with smug little smiles. Signora flushed and batted her eyelashes, as if she herself had been paid a compliment.

I looked back at Fiametta. "Who's that?" I said, my curiosity overriding the sickness in my belly.

"Why Chiara Orlandi, of course. Don't you know her? I was sure you did. She's from your hometown and until recently was under the patronage of your duke."

I'd almost forgotten. Chiara was the singer from Mantua Papà had told me about and who the duke had mentioned.

Signora gushed with pride. "That dear, angelic girl left Mantua many years ago to study music here in Venice. She's sung in Don Antonio's operas as well as in those of a good many other composers."

Fiametta couldn't restrain herself. "And now she's Maestro Tomaso's star pupil and teaching assistant. She's having her private lesson with him right now. You'll meet her later when we all go to his studio for our group lesson."

"Of course," said Signora, with moist eyes and a simper of fondness, "*I* have taught our darling Chiara almost everything she knows. But she's outstripped me. Yes indeed. She has left me far behind in her meteoric rise to the stars!"

A curious thought struck me. "That's strange. My sister and I saw Maestro Tomaso's new opera last night. If Chiara's such a singing celebrity and his star pupil, why didn't she sing in it?"

Signora gave me a hard frown, as if I'd said something impertinent.

Before she could respond, Fiametta burst in. "Oh, Chiara's not singing in any operas this winter. She's taking a break to rest her voice."

"Rest her voice?" I asked.

Ernesta, who hadn't said a word yet, held me in a steady gaze. "Yes, she sang *five* operas in a row this past season at the San Angelo and strained her throat."

Signora cleared her own throat and looked down her nose at me. "A bit of vocal strain is not unusual for a busy opera singer. Maestro Tomaso has been giving her private instruction to remedy the problem, and our dear Chiara's voice is, thank heaven, nearly restored to its former glory."

Soon after dinner I was told it was time to leave for our singing lesson. Fiametta led our little group a short distance along the Riva degli Schiavoni, past the Piazza San Marco. I gaped about at my first glimpse of Venice in full daylight.

The streets were alive with song. A man peddling roast pumpkin hawked his offerings to a melody that pulled my heartstrings. A fruit vendor warbled "Melons with hearts of fire!" and "Juicy pears that'll bathe your chin!" with so much gusto my mouth watered. Fishermen and firewood dealers melodiously cried their offerings up and down the canals, filling the briny air with cheery music.

We passed a cook shop, and the heavenly smells of roasted chicken and hot cornmeal *polenta* brought rumbles to my belly. Then we turned into a shadowy alley that led to the Campo San Moisè, and the delicious aromas and colorful sounds faded.

"Here's Maestro Tomaso's house," Fiametta told me, pointing to a dingy building that overlooked the small square.

A housekeeper led us down the front hall and into a cold, musty smelling room. The only furnishings were a harpsichord littered with music scores and a couple of armless wooden chairs. The granite floor was bare, and the grimy, unpainted plaster walls were crowded with drab looking pictures. Even in its bleakness, the room felt suffocating. My chest tightened as panic slunk in.

The other three girls huddled together, laughing and whispering. I stood alone in awkward silence.

As if out of nowhere a striking young woman, tall and blond, with catlike green eyes, seemed to float across the room. She stopped a couple of feet in front of me and looked me up and down. "You're the new girl, aren't you?"

I nodded and tried to curtsy with shaking legs.

She eyed me coolly, then glanced sidelong at the others. I heard muffled giggles.

"I am Signorina Chiara," she said. "I'm a professional opera singer and therefore a privileged member of Signora Malvolia's household." She paused, as if to give her pompous introduction of herself a chance to sink in.

Her alluring figure, encased in whalebone and silk, made me feel scrawny, homely, and insignificant.

Chiara smiled at the other three girls, turned with a

swirl of her skirts, and walked to the harpsichord.

Maestro Tomaso plodded into the room, looking tired and stern. He sat at the harpsichord and started to sift through a stack of music. Chiara stood nearby, her hands clasped in front of her. I was afraid to breathe.

The maestro fixed his eyes on me. "You there, what is your name?" he said gruffly, shifting his gaze to Chiara.

"Maestro Tomaso," she said, smiling smugly, "may I present our new student, Signorina Annina."

He looked me over with a studious frown. "We welcome you, Annina." There wasn't a trace of warmth in his stiff greeting.

His black eyes darted. "Fiametta!" he said in a quavering voice that made me startle. "Let us hear the cadenza you've been practicing."

Fiametta went to the harpsichord and turned to face the rest of us. Maestro Tomaso played a resounding chord, and she lunged into a rippling cascade of scales and trills. My mouth fell open in amazement. When she finished, every eye in the room turned to the maestro.

He stared at a score that lay open on the harpsichord rack. Finally he said, "Your scales are sloppy and your trills sound like the bleating of a goat. Return to your place, and don't make me have to listen to you again until you can manage those technical details with absolute precision."

The nostrils on Fiametta's prominent nose flared

slightly. She nodded and walked back to where she'd been standing before. I almost felt sorry for her, but strangely, she didn't seem too bothered. Out of the corner of my eye I saw her exchange an amused glance with Marzia.

One after the other, Marzia and Ernesta were called forward and subjected to similar scrutiny by the uncompromising maestro. I started to realize they were used to his harsh criticism and even expected it. No one seemed discouraged by it.

The lesson dragged on. I shifted from one foot to the other. My feet were numb from standing so long, and my back ached.

Finally Maestro Tomaso turned to Chiara. "La Signorina Orlandi will now demonstrate for you floundering songbirds her mastery of technical execution. What will you sing for us today, my dear?"

She exuded cool confidence as she glided over and murmured something to him. He scrambled through his pile of scores, laid open a thick manuscript on his rack, and waited while Chiara arranged her billowing silk skirts and revealing bodice into a stiff pose. At a nod from her he began the introduction to an aria I'd heard at his opera the night before. She soared through every note with stark precision. When she finished, the maestro's eyes glistened with fondness and awe. It was the first time I'd seen him smile.

My shrinking confidence crumbled. Chiara was obviously the kind of singer Maestro Tomaso and Don Antonio admired, and I knew I couldn't sing like that. Paolina was right. I'd fooled myself into believing in a dream that would never come true.

I didn't think I'd be asked to sing, since this was my first lesson and I hadn't had time to prepare anything. In fact, Maestro Tomaso seemed to have forgotten about me in his zeal to shower criticism on the other students and gloat over Chiara.

But Chiara hadn't forgotten me. She gave the maestro a charming smile and said, "Shouldn't we allow our new student a chance to be heard?"

I winced and wanted to protest, but didn't dare.

The maestro directed his hard gaze at me. I caught my breath.

"Yes, let us hear Signorina Annina," he said. "Annina, come forward."

The room was a haze of distorted, slow-moving images. My stomach churned painfully as my eyes drifted from Maestro Tomaso's glum face to Chiara. Her haughty half-smile twisted into a threatening sneer. My cheeks went hot with self-consciousness, and the other girls watched me with smug curiosity.

The maestro's lips were pinched. "We are almost out of time, so let us get on with this."

"Sing this," Chiara said as she shoved a score into my trembling hands.

I looked down at notes and words that were totally unfamiliar and felt a piercing twinge in my jaw. "I don't know this," I barely managed to say, in a shaky whisper.

She raised her lovely eyebrows in surprise. The slight curl of her lip and her appraising glance sharpened my feeling of dread. "Just sing it," she said. "Surely you can read music can't you?"

My heart thudded, my throat tightened in terror, and I prayed my empty stomach wouldn't start heaving. Maestro Tomaso started the introduction, and I bluffed my way through the song as best I could.

When the ordeal was finally over there was a long silence. I looked around and saw expressions of disapproval and rejection, mingled with snickering amusement. The maestro frowned and shook his head, and Chiara's pert mouth worked itself into a mocking smirk. My heart was like a stone in my chest. I wanted to turn and run, but the room's frigid atmosphere kept me frozen in place.

Maestro Tomaso had startled me earlier when he'd been so outspoken with the other singers about their less than perfect cadenzas. But the quiet control of his tone as he studied me with critical eyes was much more frightening.

"I'm sorry to have to say this, signorina, but I'm afraid your voice has serious limitations."

The muffled snickering in the room grew louder, and the maestro gave the girls a weary, ironic look. Glancing back at me he smiled with pity, then announced the end of the lesson.

I turned to Chiara with brimming eyes. There wasn't a shred of sympathy in her frosty smile. She seemed to take pleasure in my suffering.

CHAPTER 4

Il Furto

The Theft

One morning in mid February Chiara stood before me, her shapely body sheathed in an alluring blue silk gown. Every one of her golden curls was perfectly in place, and her eyes gleamed like green glass.

She looked down at me with a smile that was as icy as her emerald eyes. "We need to discuss the future of your singing instruction."

"I'd like to study with Don Antonio when he comes back to Venice," I said, feeling a little bolder than usual.

Chiara tilted her pretty head back, and her laugh was as coldly charming as her hair and figure. "Have you met him? Have you sung for him?"

"I met him in Mantua, but I haven't sung for him yet."

"You never will. Don Antonio is on an extended stay in Rome. And so, little Miss Prima Donna, you'll have to take your singing lessons with Maestro Tomaso, like the rest of us. That is, if he's willing to keep you as a student after the pathetic performances you've shown us so far."

"Why *is* Don Antonio in Rome?" My trembling voice displayed my desperation.

She shrugged. "How should I know? Probably hob-nobbing with the Pope and the rest of the Vatican luminaries. He likes to pretend he's so holy."

I felt a little rush of indignation. "Why are you talking about him like that? I thought you liked him."

"Oh? Whatever gave you that idea?"

"Well . . . haven't you sung in a lot of his operas?"

"Maybe I have. But things can change, can't they?"

Chiara's attitude toward Don Antonio was puzzling. But I had no time to dwell on that. I was too busy wondering why Papà and Paolina hadn't answered my letters. For weeks I'd been writing them, and I had yet to receive a single response. That was the worst agony of all—the agony of being cut off from my family and from everybody and everything I'd known before coming here.

I was determined not to let anyone know how miserable I felt, so I took on an attitude of defiance. This didn't help my relations with Maestro Tomaso.

One afternoon he called me to the front of the room. "Demonstrate for us the cadenza you've been practicing since our last lesson."

I was really starting to despise him. As if his gruff personality wasn't bad enough, I was noticing more and more how repulsive he was to look at. His greasy hair and bulging eyes made me cringe.

"Oh, uh," I said, struggling to come up with an excuse for why I hadn't practiced the cadenza. The truth was, the high notes he tried to make me sing made my throat feel raw and sore.

The maestro squinted at the score of vocal exercises, then turned to me. The corners of his mouth dipped. "Annina," he said, with a whining edge to his voice. "What are you waiting for? You are trying my patience."

"Yes, maestro." I stared at my shambling feet.

"Return to your place then," he said. "You're wasting my time."

He didn't ask me again to sing by myself that day, but told me to sing as softly as possible with the group. Except for an occasional half annoyed, half pitying look my way, he ignored me for the rest of the lesson.

I don't need pity! I wanted to scream at him. *I need understanding!*

THAT NIGHT I LAY on my lumpy cot, kept awake by roaring winds and rumbling thunder. After a while I crept from under my quilt, wrapped a shawl around my shoulders, and peered through the window. Biting winter air seeped into the room as pellets of hail started to beat against the glass panes, and the icy waters under my window swirled violently.

I shivered and tightened my shawl around myself. I could almost feel what it would be like to be swept into that gusty squall, and I ached to sing about that feeling. That's how I yearned to sing—to express how I felt inside about thrilling, even terrifying things.

I crawled back in bed and pressed my cheek to the cold, flat pillow. Again, I wondered why Papà and Paolina hadn't answered my pleading letters. How could they ignore my agony and condemn me to feeling so alone and abandoned? Paolina's parting words to me had been to write to her. Well I had, many times. Why wasn't she writing back?

A few days later I was in the practice room going over a set of vocal exercises Maestro Tomaso had assigned. The door opened abruptly, and I looked over to see Chiara holding a small stack of mail.

"I suppose you've been wondering about these," she said.

I bounded from the harpsichord chair and rushed to grab my letters. "Those are mine! How did you get them?"

Chiara smiled and pulled the little bundle out of my

reach. "I intercepted them."

"You can't do that!"

"Oh, but I can. Signora has entrusted me with keeping track of all the mail that comes and goes here. So I have access to every letter you try to send as well as every piece of mail that arrives for you." Her cool smile hardened into a cold, rigid line. "I've enjoyed reading the interesting things you have to say about me."

I shuddered to think what I'd written.

"Don't even think about reporting this to Signora or anyone else," she said. "If you do, I'll burn the letters and say I did it to protect you—that you were corresponding with a secret lover. Imagine what will happen to you then, when Signora tells the duke. Your ridiculous dreams will come crashing down around you like a hailstorm." Her smirking lips showed how much the prospect pleased her.

If I could have found a way to kill her at that moment I would have done it. Instead, I ran to my room, threw myself across the bed, and clenched my fists till they hurt. There was nothing I could do to protect myself from Chiara. She had me completely in her power and would keep torturing me in every way possible.

AT OUR LESSON THAT afternoon Maestro Tomaso told us about a private concert he was planning, in which we would each sing an aria. I was so excited about singing in a real performance, my feelings of hopelessness scattered like dead leaves in the winter wind.

As the big day grew closer I practiced what seemed like day and night. I went over and over the exercises the maestro had taught us, to try to build my vocal power and stretch my range. Often my throat felt like it was on fire and my voice sounded strained and hoarse. But I practiced anyway, bent on conquering my vocal shortcomings.

On the morning of the concert I washed, dressed, and rushed downstairs. We were supposed to go to Maestro Tomaso's for a rehearsal that morning, and spend the afternoon resting and getting ready for the big event. In my haste I almost ran headlong into Chiara. Her icy gaze stopped me.

"I'm afraid you won't be singing in tonight's performance," she said.

My heart jolted. "But—but why?"

She sighed, shook her head, and smiled sweetly. "I advised Maestro Tomaso to leave you out because of your pitiful lack of talent. Your vocal performances are awful. So I've decided you shouldn't be included in the concert."

"But my singing has really improved!" The shrillness of my voice rang in my ears. "I've practiced and practiced the techniques Maestro Tomaso's been teaching us, and I can sing all the arias he's taught us by heart!"

My outburst attracted the attention of the other singers. They clustered close by, eyes alert with curiosity, and I felt like the walls were closing in on me. Clinching my eyelids, I wrapped my arms around my quavering body. I ached to be protected, comforted, and told I didn't deserve such vicious treatment.

All at once my fear, rage and disappointment fused into a burst of defiance. "My singing isn't awful! I can sing better than anyone. I'll sing my aria for you now."

Chiara kept smiling while she shook her head in mock regret. She looked at the other singers and rolled her eyes, then returned her taunting gaze to me.

I braced myself and broke into the aria I'd been practicing for weeks. I felt a rush of energy as all my pain and frustrated longings surged through the music and inflamed it with fiery passion. I knew everyone here would see this out of control way of singing as a complete rebellion against conventional performance standards, but at that moment I didn't care.

Chiara interrupted me, her mouth curved in amusement. "I'm afraid we can't allow singing such as yours in our concert. After all, Maestro Tomaso has his reputation to think about." She turned to the others. "And to think the silly little creature was stupid enough to believe Don Antonio would want her as a student." Her eyes sparkled with glee, and the other girls choked with laughter.

I spun around to run to my room and felt a bony hand clutch my arm.

"Come with me, Annina," Signora said, without a drop of warmth or sympathy in her voice. She virtually dragged me to her private study and ordered me to sit. "Now," she said, after arranging herself behind her desk and fussing with her skirts. "What is all this commotion about?"

I tried to look at her, but her cold, lifeless eyes sent shivers up my back. Glancing down, I bit my lip to silence the sobs that bubbled up from my throat.

"I believe I've spoken to you before about the unacceptability of emotional outbursts in my house," she said, with a chilling lack of compassion for my misery. "It is disruptive to our routine and most disquieting for the others who reside here. I must ask you to explain yourself."

What could I say that would melt the ice in her eyes and make her understand the suffering I'd been through? Nothing. So I stayed silent, staring at my clenched hands and quivering with stifled sobs.

"Very well, Annina," she said. "If this is how you choose to behave, there will be serious consequences. I'll consider your punishment, and you will be told of my decision shortly."

I looked up and shuddered at the sight of her hard, wizened face.

"And now, I'll ask you to leave my study and return to your room, where you shall stay for the rest of the day and night, without any dinner or supper. Let your hunger be a reminder of your transgressions." She pursed her lips and turned her attention to the papers on her desk.

Shaking with humiliation and despair, I walked past the gawking stares of the others who'd been hovering outside the door, and went to my room. My mind was too drenched in pain to think clearly. I collapsed on my bed and buried my face in the cold pillow. Nothing would ever be right in my life again. The world had turned against me. I might as well be in hell. Hell could be no worse than this.

CHAPTER 5

La Punizione

The Punishment

By evening my belly squirmed with hunger, and I felt like I was being eaten alive by anguish. I clenched my tear-drenched pillow as the same baffling questions kept tormenting my mind: Why does Chiara hate me? Why is she so determined to see me fail? And most mystifying of all, why does everybody worship her so much? Her strange power terrified me.

The next day Chiara pulled me aside and taunted me about the concert I'd been excluded from the night before. "You should have heard us. We were superb. Of course, *you* will never experience the kind of ecstasy that comes from being caught in the magic of such glorious music. Your pathetic lack of talent will prevent that." The corners of her mouth curled in an ugly, distorted way.

I forced myself to swallow my fury, and with as much dignity as I could muster walked with the others to Maestro Tomaso's house.

He trudged into the music room in his usual gloomy way, and his eyes fell on me. "*Well*, Annina."

I straightened, startled. My knees trembled.

His face was steely. "Have you learned your lesson? Did an evening without supper, banned from the company of your fellow singing students, teach you to obey your superiors? Are you ready to accept your humble lot as the most incompetent singer in my studio?"

"Yes, maestro," I said, trying not to show my distress.

"Very well then."

I caught a glimpse of Chiara's smug smile and felt my cheeks burn. Why was Maestro Tomaso being so hateful? He'd always been stern and blunt, but never this mean. Chiara must be working on him, I thought. She has the maestro twisted around her little finger just like she has everyone else.

From the corner of my eye I saw the other singers glaring at me. It didn't matter. Today I was determined to be a model of confidence and poise. I ignored the whispers and sly glances and acted like nothing unpleasant had ever happened to me. This seemed to have some effect. The maestro even gave me one or two approving looks, and Chiara seemed stumped for ways to get me riled.

After our lesson she found a way.

"Annina, dear," she said with crafty sweetness as I hurried past her. "Not so fast."

I turned to her, my eyebrows raised and my smile forced.

"Signora asked me to inform you of your punishment for yesterday's outrageous outburst. You'll receive no coal for a month. Your *scaldino*," she said, caressing the word almost obscenely with her tongue, "will stay empty and cold. Have a *frigid* night's sleep." Her frosty smile matched her words.

THAT NIGHT I SHIVERED under my thin quilt and listened to the February winds roar. My fingers were too stiff to move. My *scaldino*, the ceramic pot that sat on top of the trunk at the foot of my bed, and should have been filled with glowing hot charcoal, lay empty—a gaping reminder of my undeserved punishment.

Again, nagging thoughts racked my mind. Why was I the victim of so much unjust treatment? For some reason Chiara had a grudge against me. And she had a lot of power over this little world she'd created for herself. But I couldn't imagine why. What made her so special? Was it that she was beautiful and talented and Maestro Tomaso's star singing pupil? Why did everybody like her so much and give her everything she wanted? Even Don Antonio had given her leading roles in some of his operas. How could a nice person like him put up with a cunning witch like her?

The next day Chiara cornered me after our midday meal. She carried a score, and her face was smug. "You might as well accept that you'll never be a singer. But that doesn't mean you can't be useful. Here's a motet Don Antonio wrote before he left for Rome. I want you to copy it and transpose it up a tone. I have to sing the motet at Vespers this Sunday evening, and I need it in a higher key. Have it done by three this afternoon."

"I won't have time to finish it before our singing lesson. If I do the copying now I'll be late."

"I suppose that means you must work all the faster. I want the score delivered to my room by three o'clock sharp."

"Please, Chiara, I don't think I can do it that fast. Can't I start now and finish later? If I'm late Maestro Tomaso will be very angry, and I'm in enough trouble with him as it is."

"That's your problem, not mine. If you weren't so slow and inept you'd have no trouble at all. Complete the copy like I've asked, or I'll have you expelled from the maestro's studio. Have I made myself clear?"

"Yes," I muttered.

The copying was tedious, but I worked frantically. It wouldn't have been so hard if I didn't have to transpose the key. Not only did every note have to be changed, I also had to redo all the sharps and flats. It didn't help that Don Antonio seemed to use some kind of shorthand for the sharps and flats. Obviously he didn't have the patience to write them in either.

I ran my fingers over the original score and longed to savor these notes he'd penned with his own hand. But there was no time to linger and daydream. I copied as fast as I could, but by two o'clock I was only a little more than halfway through. I kept going at a furious pace and barely managed to finish the task by three o'clock. Then I rushed the score, both the original and my copy, to Chiara's room before dashing off to singing class. I had to creep out of the house since Signora would be furious if she knew I was walking through the dark *calli* alone.

I tried to sneak in the studio without being seen, but the maestro spotted me. He brought the lesson to a halt and glowered at me.

"Annina, what do you mean entering my class at this late hour?" he said in his irritating nasal tone, his loose jowls quivering.

"I'm sorry, maestro," I said, cringing.

"Sorry are you? This won't do at all. Be silent, and I'll deal with you later."

The other students flung smirking, slantwise glances at me, and even though I was late the lesson seemed like it would never end.

Finally the maestro dismissed the class. Then he turned to me with a piercing glare. "Annina, stay where you are," he said, while the snickering little cluster of singers got ready to leave.

My cheeks were in flames, and I felt pinpricks deep inside.

After the others left, the maestro ordered me to come forward. "This is absolutely the last straw, signorina. I suppose it's not enough for you to subject us to your musical ineptitude. Now you've demonstrated that you have no respect for the rules of my studio. Worst of all, you've shown that you have no appreciation for the privileges you've been granted despite your lack of talent. You have forced me to make an example of you so my other students will see that disregard for rules and decorum will not be tolerated."

My heart thumped and my knees went weak. I wanted to tell him this was all Chiara's fault, but I knew that wouldn't do any good. She'd lured Maestro Tomaso into her slippery schemes, just like she'd lured Signora Malvolia and everyone in her household.

He went on. "I'll discuss the situation with Signorina Chiara and she will inform you of our decision."

Later that evening Chiara showed up at my bedroom door with a smirk of triumph. "I've recommended to Maestro Tomaso that you be expelled from his studio, and he's agreed. So you're no longer a singing student and will be confined to this house until further notice."

I seethed with hidden rage and thought how much I hated that disgusting little man who reminded me so much of a twanging toad!

"Also, I've requested further punishment for your botched job on Don Antonio's score. Because of your carelessness and incompetence I'll have to pay someone more skilled to copy the score again. So I've asked Signora to reassign your status in this household to that of a servant. Tomorrow morning you'll begin to learn the art of dressmaking and assist our resident seamstress in sewing operatic costumes. That will be your fulltime job."

CRUSHING LONELINESS HAUNTED ME through the night. My heart ached for home. But Mamma had abandoned me, and Papà and Paolina had sent me to live with cruel strangers. My worst fear had come true. There wasn't a single person in my life who cared about me at all.

I crept to the foot of my cot and for the first time since I'd arrived at Signora's house pulled *la moretta* from my trunk. Gazing into her empty eyes, I pleaded softly. "Save me, *moretta.* The whole world has turned against me. You're my only hope. *La chiromante* said you'd shield me from suffering. Please shield me now."

But you won't silence me, I vowed inwardly, pressing *la moretta* to my aching heart. *I will not be silenced!*

CHAPTER 6

La Cucitrice

The Seamstress

Bleary-eyed and sluggish, I reported next morning to the sewing room. Pausing outside the door, I warily glimpsed the cramped space, crowded with bolts of colorful fabrics, piles of dress patterns, bobbins of thread, and baskets overflowing with needles, pinkers, and bodkins. My heart turned over and sank. The dreaded task I'd managed to avoid back in Mantua was now taking over my life. And this time there was no escape.

"*Benvenuta*, Annina, welcome!"

The seamstress's smiling round face, moist with sweat, lit up the cluttered little room. She was the same young woman whose friendly smile had comforted me my first day at Signora Malvolia's.

"*Grazie*," I said, dropping a quick curtsy.

She waved her hand, as if she were batting away a fly. "There's no need for ceremony with me. I'm not one of those puffed up singers. I only make their dresses and costumes. My name's Graziana."

She sat behind a long worktable, busy with needle and thread. I couldn't stop gazing into her pale blue eyes. They glittered like ponds in the sunlight and seemed to absorb and reflect everything around her.

"Well sit down," she said, nodding toward the stool across the table. Her eyes darted around the room. "As you can see, I'm long overdue for some help here."

"I'm afraid I won't be much help." I nervously slid onto the stool, my shoulders tense. "I'm not very good at sewing."

"Don't worry," she said, leaning across the table with a sly smile. "I'll only give you the easy work. Nobody needs to know. Now why don't you cut out this *scialletto* for me."

She handed me a short length of white muslin with the paper pattern already pinned to it, and a pair of scissors. I snipped around the simple neck-piece outline and felt my shoulders start to relax.

"There, that's painless, isn't it?" Graziana said, her smile turning cozy.

I nodded and tried to smile back.

She peered at me with puckered lips. "You've hardly

said a word since you came in here. Are you always this quiet?"

"No, not always," I said, my cheeks warming.

Her lips eased back into a smile. "So tell me, what's a little thing like you doing all alone in Venice? You can't be more than twelve."

The heat rose in my cheeks as I glanced down at my barely budding breasts. "Actually, I'm fourteen."

"Well aren't you lucky to still be so slender. By the time I was fourteen I was round as a barrel!" She laughed good-naturedly.

I laughed with her, and the weight of my embarrassment lifted. "Truthfully I'd rather be plump." I thought of Chiara's lush bosom. "Men seem to like that."

"That all depends. I'm twenty-two and I still haven't snagged one."

"Oh you will, Graziana," I said, not wanting to spoil her cheerful mood. "You're so friendly and kind. I'm sure you'll find an *amico* soon."

"And is that why you're here, Annina?" she said, her eyes bright with interest. "In search of love?"

If only she knew how close she was to the truth. But the love my heart craved had nothing to do with romance. I hesitated a moment, then took a deep breath. "I came to Venice to study singing with a certain teacher."

"Oh? Who's that?"

"A famous violinist and opera impresario . . . they call

him *il Prete Rosso.*" I bit my lip, waiting for her to laugh in disbelief.

But she didn't laugh. "Ah," she said, turning her eyes back to her sewing.

She knew something, I could feel it. I also sensed Graziana was not someone who could hold gossip in for long. I waited for her to go on, but she kept her eyes on her sewing and said nothing.

"When I got here a few weeks ago, he'd just left for Rome," I finally said. "I have no idea why."

"Mmm."

My heart beat anxiously. "Graziana, do you know why he left Venice?"

She glanced up at me with a shrewd gleam in her eye. "I guess you haven't heard. He had to leave Venice after his last opera here. *La verità*—something, I think."

"*La verità in cimento*?"

"Yes, that's it. The Contested Truth, interesting title. How did you know about it?"

"My patron, the duke, told me about that opera right before Don Antonio left Mantua. But what did *La verità* have to do with his leaving Venice?"

"*Well.*" She sucked in her lips and her eyes grew brighter. "You know how the singers here talk. I heard he felt forced to leave because of the vicious pamphlet that got passed around about him and his new opera soon after its first performance."

"Who wrote the pamphlet and what did it say?"

"A nobleman named Benedetto Marcello. He fancies himself a composer, and his family are part owners of the San Angelo Theater. Anyway, he decided *La verità* was too exotic and wrote a nasty satire about it, called *Il Teatro alla moda*, The Theater of Fashion. In it he makes fun of everything about *La verità*. Marcello thinks opera should be stuffy and dignified and feels *il Prete Rosso*'s works are too unconventional. The pamphlet spread like wildfire and caused a huge stir."

"But I thought Don Antonio's operas were very popular in Venice."

"Annina, when you've lived here long enough you'll see that Venetians love anything that's new and different. But they're also fickle and change their tastes as often as they change their Carnival masks. A lampoon from a bigwig like Marcello can make them flip-flop faster than you can blink."

I fumed inwardly. How unfair! Don Antonio's operas are brilliant. It was obvious he poured so much of himself into his music, which was what gave it the power to captivate me. If he worried about boring "convention," his music wouldn't have that power. Then I had a surprising thought. *He's like me.* I don't like convention either. I feel stifled and frustrated by it. Now I realized he and I had to put up with the same kind of injustice. This made me even more determined to stick to my convictions and not let Chiara or anyone else bully me.

But there was no escape from Chiara's taunting. Some days she seemed to be lurking around every corner, waiting for a chance to lord it over me. One night I silently cried myself to sleep after she showed up at my bedside to jeer about the stolen letters she still hoarded. Graziana noticed my red eyes the next morning, and after a little prompting I poured out my feelings about Chiara.

"Why is she so hateful to me?" I asked.

"Because as she sees it you took away her main source of income and knocked her down a peg besides."

"Why would she think that?"

Graziana looked up from her sewing and raised her eyebrows. "Isn't it obvious? She'd been under the patronage of the Duke of Massa Carrara since she first came to Venice, but early last month he decided to drop her."

My lips parted as I gave a little gasp. "That's when he wrote my father and offered to pay for me to come here."

She smiled knowingly. "Now you're catching on."

I thought about this a moment. "How long *has* Chiara been in Venice, Graziana?"

"About five years, far as I know. That's how long she's lived at Signora Malvolia's anyway, which is almost as long as I've been here."

"What was she like when you first knew her?"

"She poured on the charm with anybody she thought she could manipulate. She's good at that."

At that moment Marzia came in with a dress to be altered. Graziana put down her sewing and went to see what was needed. The interruption ended our discussion. I'd have to wait for another opportunity to hear the rest of the story about Chiara.

THE NEXT MORNING Graziana and I found ourselves alone again.

"Please, Graziana," I said, "finish what you started to say yesterday about Chiara. Why does she have so much power here?"

She cupped her hand around her mouth and leaned across the table. "There's a rumor that the people who raised her in Mantua adopted her as an infant, and that her real mother is Bianca Stramponi, one of the most beautiful courtesans in Venice. All the rich nobles hanker for her. Nobody's supposed to know Chiara's her bastard daughter, but I've heard it whispered."

"What's a courtesan?"

"*Dio mio*, Annina, how have you managed to stay so innocent? A courtesan is a charming, highly cultivated woman who makes her living granting favors to wealthy men. Venice is teaming with them."

"What kinds of favors?"

"Hasn't anyone ever told you anything? The kinds of

favors courtesans show their male clients have to do with romance and lovemaking."

"*Oh*," I said, blushing.

Graziana leaned closer, eyes darting. "But let me tell you more about Chiara. They say her father's a rich Austrian nobleman and a great patron of the opera. He also likes to have his way with the ladies. I've heard he even had a romance with Signora Malvolia years ago, before he jilted her and left her *senza quattrini*, penniless."

I could hardly contain my hilarity. It was impossible to imagine Signora having a romance with anyone, least of all a wealthy nobleman.

Graziana shared my barely suppressed mirth. "I know, it sounds ridiculous. But apparently Signora was quite a siren in her younger days, and that's how she lured the rich Austrian into sponsoring her opera career. Though now that she's old and dried out and no man will so much as look at her, she's turned bitter as wormwood." She giggled. "Anyway, when Chiara first came here she used to brag to everyone that her father was a powerful prince who'd one day appear to launch her on a great operatic career."

"Did she really believe he would?"

"She used to believe it. But when so much time went by and he never showed up, she lost hope. That's when she started to turn nasty."

"But that doesn't explain why Chiara has so much

control around here."

"Don't you see, Annina? Signora is a sour old maid, reduced to running a boarding house after a glamorous stage career. She knows Chiara's father is the lover and patron who abandoned her. And just like Chiara, she's fooled herself into believing that if and when he comes back he'll take her away from all this. Ha! Wouldn't that be the day?"

I LAY AWAKE for a long time that night and thought about the things Graziana had told me. I had a better idea now why Chiara had so much power, and I knew I'd have to be very careful around her. She had important people on her side, and she'd be sure to ruin any chance I might have of following my dream.

Gloom shrouded me. Nothing was turning out as I'd hoped.

CHAPTER 7

Mercoledì delle Ceneri

Ash Wednesday

It was Ash Wednesday, and Signora let me walk the few steps from our door to the Church of the Pietà for Mass. No one else wanted to go.

I pulled my shawl over my head before I entered the church. Inside the door, I dipped my fingers in holy water and made the sign of the cross. The Pietà's all female chorus and orchestra, the *figlie di coro*, were already in the choir loft, barely visible behind the wrought-iron balcony grille that protected them from public view. Each girl wore a red dress, symbolizing, I'd been told, the Pietà's mission of "mercy." They sat in silence.

I savored the peacefulness. The altar was bathed in candlelight that flickered and bounced off the whitewashed stone walls and gave the entire sanctuary a mystical radiance. The rich scent of incense flooded my nostrils, and in spite of the frigid air, warmth enfolded me.

Then I noticed heads turn. A sandy-haired man, with violin case in one hand and a large portfolio and round-brimmed hat under his other arm, had just come in through the main door. He hurried toward the choir loft stairs. My mouth fell open and my heart almost jolted from my chest when I realized who it was.

He wore a priestly black cassock, and a dark cloak hung from his shoulders. Transfixed, I watched him disappear up the stairs.

The liturgy began with a solemn chant, in Latin, that seemed to be sung by voices of angels from above.

Exaudi nos, Domine,
quoniam benigna est
misericordia tua.

Hear us, O Lord,
for thy mercy is kind.

For a moment the heavenly voices, the incense, and the coldness of the marble tiles under my feet made me light-headed. I could feel my heart pelting my breastbone. Squeezing my eyes shut to steady myself, I prayed I'd have a chance to speak to him before he left.

At the end of Mass the red-clad *figlie di coro*, some carrying instruments, filed down the stairs and out the main door. A faint cross of ashes clung to each of their foreheads. The congregation had already dispersed, and I was alone, shivering in the darkening sanctuary. Specks fell into my eyes from my own smudge of ashes and I tried to flick them away with icy fingers.

I heard footsteps on the stairs. Closing my eyes, I prayed silently: *Please, God, let it be him.* When I opened my eyes he'd reached the foot of the staircase. He paused, set his violin case and leather folder on the floor and threw his cloak over his shoulders. With his violin in his left hand and his scores and hat under his other arm, he headed for the main door. I scurried after him.

"Don Antonio!"

He turned, and his blue eyes gazed into my dark ones.

Would he remember me? My heart thudded in my ears as I crept closer to him. I pulled my shawl away from my face and felt it slip from my head.

He squinted, then his face lit up. "Annina?"

"Yes, it's me," I said, bobbing a curtsy with trembling knees.

"*Annina.* Why, I almost didn't recognize you. How long has it been?" His warm smile and gentle, fluid Venetian accent tickled my heart.

"Only a few months," I said, trying to steady my shaking voice.

"And here you are in Venice. I had no idea. When did you arrive?"

"About four weeks ago. The Duke of Massa Carrara is paying for me to live and study here."

"Is that so?" His smile dimmed slightly. "Who are you studying with?"

"Maestro Tomaso Albinoni. I'd hoped to study with you, but you were in Rome when I got here."

"Oh, I see. Where are you living, Annina?"

"Near here, at Signora Malvolia's boardinghouse."

"Well, that's on the way to my house. Come, I'll walk you home. They're probably wondering where you are."

He moved his violin to his right hand and held the heavy wooden door for me. Outside, he placed his black clerical hat on his head. I was disappointed not to have more time to talk to him. I wanted to pour out all my hurt and frustration, but I didn't know where to begin.

The sun was going down and the dark green waters of the San Marco Canal glowed in the evening twilight. Ash Wednesday marked the beginning of Lent and the end of the Carnival season, so the streets and canals were now quiet and almost deserted.

"How are your studies going, Annina?" he asked.

The frosty air made my lips feel stiff and set my whole body trembling. I stopped and stared at the cold gray blocks of pavement, blinking hard to cool my burning eyes. He waited. I knew I had to say something.

My eyes met his. "All right, I suppose," I said, and my voice broke.

His face clouded with concern. He moved his violin to his other hand and put a comforting arm around me. "Tell me what's troubling you," he said.

Something deep inside me stirred, then melted, and tears came. "Maestro Tomaso doesn't think I have the voice to sing opera. He and his other students are always putting down my singing, even though I practice all the time and try my best to get better. And now he's angry with me for being late and has expelled me from his singing class." I choked on my last words and couldn't say any more.

He squeezed his arm around me a little tighter. It seemed so long since anyone had touched me affectionately I'd almost forgotten how it felt. I leaned into him and clutched the edge of his cloak. His clothes smelled faintly of spicy incense mixed with the scent of the brisk evening air. I wanted to melt into his warmth.

But suddenly I was ashamed of my undignified behavior and forced myself to pull away from him. I sniffled and wiped my nose with the back of my hand. My teeth started to chatter, and my fingers stung from the cold. He reached in his pocket and handed me his handkerchief.

"I'm sorry for making such a scene," I said, flushing and dabbing tears.

"You've had a hard time of it so far," he said quietly.

"I understand why you feel so distraught. I only wish I'd been here to help you." Then his voice brightened. "I'll tell you what, Annina. Why don't you come to my house tomorrow afternoon for a lesson? I'll send someone to fetch you."

"You mean, you want me to study with you? Even after what Maestro Tomaso said about my voice?"

"*Non importa*, that doesn't matter. Tomaso's old-fashioned and his concept of theatrical singing is limited. Besides, the poor wretch has been in a state of gloom since his wife died last year. So you mustn't take what he's told you to heart, Annina. What's important is that you *do* have a natural flair for drama. I sensed that the first time I laid eyes on you. I can teach you everything you need to know about singing technique."

His smile was reassuring, and I felt like an oppressive weight had been lifted from my shoulders. I blinked back my tears and shared his smile.

We were in front of Signora's house, and she appeared at the door. "Annina, there you are! I told you to come home immediately after—"she started to scold, until she spotted Don Antonio.

Her eyelids fluttered with surprise. "Don Antonio! What an unexpected pleasure."

"*Buona sera*, Signora Malvolia. It's all right, Annina's been with me."

"Has she, indeed?" She looked astounded.

"*Sì.* And I'm glad to have the opportunity to inform you myself, Signora, that I've asked Annina to come to my house for singing lessons, starting tomorrow afternoon. I'll send a gondolier around for her at four o'clock."

"Well . . . I—" she began to stammer.

He silenced her with a charming smile and tipped his hat. "It's been a pleasure, Signora. *Buona notte*, Annina. *A domani*, I'll see you tomorrow."

"*A domani*, Don Antonio," I said breathlessly, hardly able to believe my good fortune.

I HURRIED TO MY ROOM, giddy with excitement. Tossing my shawl across the bed, I realized I still clutched Don Antonio's handkerchief in my trembling hand. I held it to my nose and savored once more his salty, fiery scent. Tingling euphoria spread through my body.

"So," came a sharp voice from the doorway, startling me back to my senses. Chiara stood at the door with pursed lips. "It seems you're craftier than I'd suspected. You've managed to use your artful wiles to persuade Don Antonio to give you a private lesson. I would never have believed this audacity even of *you*, little Miss Annina."

How in the world did she know? No doubt Signora couldn't wait to report to her.

"I didn't try to persuade him," I said. "It was his idea."

"Indeed?"Chiara's pursed lips hardened into a smirk. "And just what do you think could have caused him to have such an absurd idea?"

"He knows my father. My father worked with his opera company in Mantua. I met him there and he remembers me."

"Ah. But he's never heard you try to sing, has he?"

"Not yet."

"Of course he hasn't. Would he be insane enough to throw away his time on you if he had? Now think about this, you sly little imp. How will he feel about you when he realizes you've finagled him into wasting his valuable time?"

"I don't think he's going to feel that way," I said, not too convincingly.

"Oh no? I think you're wrong. So I've decided to do you a favor. I'll go to Don Antonio in advance and warn him about you. I'll be there when you arrive for your lesson. I'll remind him that you're just a foolish little girl and do my best to shield you from his annoyance."

Her smile was so sickeningly sweet I felt like gagging.

CHAPTER 8

La Lettera Segreta

The Secret Letter

That night I tossed restlessly in bed. In spite of Chiara's threats, I was glowing with so much happiness over my unexpected meeting with Don Antonio I almost didn't notice the room's icy chill. I just *had* to tell somebody about it. But who could I tell? No one, not even Graziana. As much as I trusted her, I'd die before I admitted to her how his comforting touch made me feel.

I'll write a letter to Paolina, I decided. I've always been able to tell her anything. Eagerly I lit a candle and rifled through my trunk for paper, quill pen, and ink. My fingers brushed the velvety darkness of *la moretta*. "Please don't let Chiara ruin things for me," I whispered. But I left the mask in the trunk and closed the lid. I didn't want to hide behind *la moretta*, and I wouldn't be muzzled.

Back in bed with my lapboard, I started to pour out my feelings:

Dear Paolina,

Tonight something absolutely wonderful has happened! After a wretched, miserable month here at Signora Malvolia's house, Don Antonio has come back into my life. How can I express how he makes me feel? I'm tingling inside so much I can't sleep. I can't stop thinking about how I felt when he put his arm around me. And the way he looked at me, his eyes full of tenderness and understanding.

The memory is so delicious I feel like I'm melting inside, over and over again. He's a burst of sunshine after a month of cold, rainy gloom!

I'll stop now, because I don't know what else to say. I want to be well rested for my lesson with him tomorrow. But how can I sleep? I'm too happy to sleep. I just want to keep reliving the sweetness of those few moments with him.

Your Loving Sister,
Annina

My heart fluttered softly as I folded the letter and hid it in my trunk. I knew I'd never mail it. But writing it felt good. It helped define my feelings and put them in a safe, private place. I'd be able to read and relive those feelings in secret anytime I wanted.

This would be *la mia lettera segreta*, my secret letter.

THE NEXT DAY the gondolier arrived promptly at four. Chiara was nowhere in sight, and I shuddered to think what she might be up to.

The boat ride was brief, just a short distance up the Canale San Marco, and down a series of narrow side canals to the *Ponte del Paradiso*, Paradise Bridge. I could have easily walked there myself. But it was considered improper for a girl to be out on the streets of Venice alone, even for short distances.

My insides felt as agitated as the canal waters that churned in the winter wind. What would Don Antonio think of my singing? What if I disappointed him, like I'd disappointed everyone else?

The gondolier helped me from the boat, and I knocked at the door overlooking the canal. My heart raced.

A slender woman answered. "You must be Annina."

"*Sì*, signora."

She seemed close to Don Antonio's age and had his reddish blond hair and warm, inviting smile. "Please come in, Annina. I'm Margarita, Antonio's sister," she said, taking my hand. "He's with someone, but he's expecting you. Follow me, dear."

Margarita's friendliness eased my agitation, but I was still nervous about the lesson. I was also embarrassed about my childish behavior the night before. How could I expect him to take me seriously when I'd carried on like a frantic little girl?

The door of the room where Margarita led me was ajar. She knocked lightly, pushed it open, and smiled at me. "Go right in, Annina."

"*Grazie*, signora," I said, with a quick curtsy.

The room was fragrant with the mingled aromas of polished mahogany and old books. Sunlight poured through sparkling windows, illuminating the parquet floor and filling the room with a warm glow. Don Antonio stood by a credenza examining a page of music and didn't notice me at first. I gazed at him as his critical eyes scanned the score.

My racing heart faltered. It was *my* score he held in his hand—the motet Chiara had made me copy, which had gotten me into so much trouble. And true to her word, Chiara stood near the harpsichord, glaring at me with cool green eyes and a smile of satisfaction. Her voluptuous, tightly corseted figure and womanly poise made me feel skinny and gawky. My knees started to quake.

After what seemed like an endless moment, Don Antonio looked up from the score. His eyes met mine, and his face brightened. "*Salve*, Annina. Thank you for coming." He glanced at Chiara. "*Grazie*, signorina, that will be all."

She looked flustered for an instant but quickly arranged her face into a charming simper. "Oh, but maestro, as Annina's friend I feel I should stay and offer her my support."

His smile faded, and there was an edge to his voice. "If you're so supportive of her, then why did you deliberately undermine her studies?"

Chiara looked taken aback. "I?—undermine her studies? What a thing to say, maestro. As I've already explained, Maestro Tomaso decided Annina should be punished for her careless work on your score, and for her tardiness. I tried to intercede for her, but he insisted on it. It's not her fault of course, poor little thing. It was foolish of her to think she could handle the rigors of musical training here in Venice."

Tense and wide-eyed, I shifted my gaze from Chiara to Don Antonio.

He gave her a stern look. "Signorina Annina is not in training to be a copyist. If you hadn't forced her to do work she's not responsible for she wouldn't have been late. I've already spoken to Tomaso about this, and I think I have an idea what actually happened. Now if you'll kindly excuse us." His tone left no room for argument.

She raised her chin, but I noticed her lip tremble. I managed with difficulty to keep the corners of my own lips from curling up.

"Oh, and one more thing, Chiara," he said as she approached the door.

She turned and gave him a half wounded, half questioning look.

"I trust you'll make sure Signorina Annina has sufficient coal. It's not healthy to sleep in an unheated room in this dank weather."

Without a word, Chiara gave him a quick nod and cast me a stinging glance before she swept out of the room.

Don Antonio looked at me with an encouraging smile. "Well, Annina, what would you like to sing for me?"

I finally let my mouth curl into a grin. "I'd like to sing an aria you wrote, *Quanto m'alletta.*"

"Ah, Cleonilla's Act I aria from *Ottone in Villa*, my very first opera. Let me see, though. I'm not sure where I put the score." He went to the credenza and started looking through a pile of manuscripts.

"It's all right," I said. "I don't need the music."

"No? Then we'll both make do with our memories."

He sat at the harpsichord and played the aria's introduction. My throat tightened, and I had a hard time taking a deep enough breath. But my fear started to dissolve as soon as I began to sing.

How alluring is the dewy grass,
how pleasing that pretty flower.
The perfume of one is fragrant with love,
the green of the other
fills my tender heart with hope.

When the aria was over, Don Antonio looked like he was deep in thought. He sighed and frowned.

My heart flurried.

"Annina," he said finally, "you sing with much sincerity and conviction. But there are some problems with your technique."

A sinking feeling swept over me. I bit my lip and stared at the floor.

"Now, now," he hastened to add, "it's nothing to be disturbed about. Your technical problems are quite fixable. Here, let me show you."

He stood and came over to me. "First of all, your jaw is much too tight." He touched the sides of my face very lightly. "Relax your jaw, and your throat will open up as well."

I felt the hardness of his left-hand fingertips, toughened by years of furious violin playing. It felt nice. My jaw loosened, and the tightness in my face and throat started to ease a little.

"Very good," he said. "Now the other problem we need to address is your breathing. You're inhaling in a shallow way, from your chest, so you can't get in enough air to sustain a full, rounded tone. You need to breathe from here. May I?"

I had no idea what he meant to do, but I nodded.

He stepped to my side, put his left hand on my shoulder, and placed the palm of his right hand just below my ribs. "Push my hand out while you breathe in slowly, and keep your shoulders relaxed."

I inhaled and felt the gentle pressure of his hand. I was stiff and nervous at first, but soon my breathing fell into a comfortable rhythm.

"*Eccellente*," he said. "Excellent." He went back to the harpsichord and played a single note. "Drop your jaw, breathe like I showed you, and sing this note on 'ah'."

Trying hard to remember everything he'd told me, I sang the note very softly.

"*Bene*, good. Now let's see if we can make it even better." He took up his violin and bowed the same note, this time drawing out the sound in a long, pulsating tone. "Close your eyes and try to match the sound of the violin, Annina. Pretend you *are* the violin."

He played the note again, and my voice and the violin's sad tremolo became a single sound. He played down a tone, and my voice moved with it effortlessly. He continued moving down, then back up to higher and higher notes.

Finally he put down his violin. "I hear tremendous improvement already. Let's try the aria again."

He went back to the harpsichord, and I repeated the aria.

"That was so much better," he said when I was finished. "But I hear now another difficulty. The piece is too high for you. Your natural voice is centered in a lower range. Try again in a different key."

He started the introduction once more, in a lower key. I glided into the opening notes, and the little bit of tension that was still in my throat and jaw evaporated into velvety comfort. My voice sailed through the aria with more ease, and more pleasure, than I'd ever thought possible.

"*Brava*, that was wonderful, Annina. Despite what anyone has told you, you must understand that your technical shortcomings have nothing to do with your inner talent. The difficulties you've been experiencing are merely external problems that are quite separate from your natural abilities and can be overcome with study and practice."

A thrill stirred in me.

He stood and began to pace the room. "Now I'll tell you what really impresses me about your singing. You sing with a heartfelt fervor that brings the emotional meaning of the aria to life. That's something that can't be taught. Many singers act as if technical perfection is an end in itself and have no sensitivity for the real substance of opera. They don't understand that technique is just a tool for expressing the feelings within. Opera is drama, not a display of vocal skills. You have a natural aptitude for manifesting emotional depth, which is the true essence of drama, and that's a priceless gift."

My heart flurried, only this time it wasn't from fear. I felt my face light up with a brilliant smile.

He paused in his pacing and smiled with me. "*Dimmi*, Annina, tell me. How do you know this aria?"

"My mother used to sing it with me. But she went away and took her music scores with her." My voice grew a little unsteady, but I tried hard to keep smiling. "It's all right, though, because I can sing all her music by heart."

His gaze was steady and kind, and a comforting feeling spread through me.

I RETURNED TO SIGNORA'S HOUSE feeling happier than I'd felt in a long time. I ran to my room, lay on my bed and hugged my pillow, overjoyed to see my *scaldino* had already been filled with fresh coal.

Then I heard the rustle of silk and light footsteps in the hall. I jolted to a sitting position.

Chiara stood in the doorway, smirking. "I suppose you're feeling rather good about yourself."

Unsure where this was leading, I waited to hear what she'd say next.

"You've managed to take full advantage of Don Antonio's good nature, and now you think you're on top of the world. You think he'll solve all your problems and your foolish dreams will at last come true. Correct me if

I'm wrong." Her smirking mouth hardened into a grim, lifeless smile.

"I haven't thought anything like that," I said, trying to calm the tremor in my throat. "Don Antonio only told me that I have a lot of dramatic potential."

"Did he now? And how will he feel about your dramatic potential when I inform him you've been writing secret letters that tell all about your crazed infatuation with him?"

I barely managed a pinched whisper. "*What?* How do you know about that letter?"

"Because I've so enjoyed reading it." Her hard smile became a sneer. "Private correspondence can be so deliciously revealing."

I lunged for my trunk and groped through it with shaking hands.

"Don't bother," she said. "I have it."

She pulled the letter from her bodice and opened it, as her face froze into a mask of mock fascination. "Let's see, it's all so interesting. Ah, here's an especially intriguing passage: *I'm tingling inside so much that I can't sleep. I can't stop thinking about the sensation of his arm around me. And the way he looked at me, his eyes full of tenderness and understanding. The memory is so delicious I feel like I'm melting inside, over and over again.*" Chiara's sneering smile worked its way into a harassing grin.

"Give it to me!" I rushed to grab the letter from her. I

wanted to shake her senseless. I wanted to scratch her eyes out!

"Oh my," she said, stepping back and holding up her free hand. "Throwing a tantrum will get us nowhere, will it? This fascinating little gem is perfectly safe—for now. And if you're a good girl and do exactly as I say, I'll try to see that it doesn't fall into the wrong hands." She tucked the letter into her bodice and left the room.

I groped through my trunk for *la moretta.* Yes, she was still there! Trembling with stifled sobs I pressed her to my face and clenched the *bottone* between my teeth.

I might as well be mute, I wailed silently. Chiara now has the power not only to humiliate me but to make Don Antonio lose all respect for me. I'll have to do whatever she says. I can't risk having him see that letter.

CHAPTER 9

La Verità

The Truth

The next day, I wondered how I'd get through my singing lesson. Chiara's threats clutched my heart like a vise. I wanted to tell Don Antonio what she'd done to me so he could make things right again. But I knew if I said a word to him about her she'd somehow find out and make things worse than they already were.

I stood outside his studio and heard the sweet strain of his violin from behind the door. Determined to put Chiara out of my mind, I took a deep breath and knocked boldly. The sound of the violin tapered to a halt, and he invited me in.

Maybe my smile was too fixed. He seemed to notice something, and his pleasant expression faded to a look of concern. "Are you all right?" he asked.

"Oh, I'm fine." My voice didn't sound like my own. There was a false brightness to it.

He didn't look convinced. "You don't have to tell me what's wrong if you don't want to. But I'd like you to channel the feeling you're experiencing into your singing. I want you to sing that feeling."

My cheeks ached from my forced smile, and I blinked hard to keep tears from spilling.

"Do you know this aria, *Solo quella guancia bella*?" He handed me a score. "It's from one of my recent operas, *La verità in cimento*."

"Oh," I said, my interest roused. "I've heard a lot about that opera, but I don't know the music."

I held the score in front of me and squinted through blurry eyes.

Only that beautiful,
charming proud face
has my love and mercy.

Taking a deep breath, I tried to concentrate on the things Don Antonio had taught me the day before—to relax my jaw and breathe from below my ribs. Before I knew it the aria was streaming from my throat, and I felt something close to ecstasy. The sobs that had threatened to spurt out turned into glorious musical sounds, and I was carried to a world far away from Chiara and her threats. The aria ended, but the spellbinding truth, the astonishing candor, of Don Antonio's music kept singing in my heart.

He looked at me steadily. "Whatever it is that's hurting you is fueling your singing with a dramatic immediacy that's truly extraordinary."

I shook with excitement. "Do you really think so?"

"*Assolutamente*, Annina, absolutely. You have a rare ability to fill your musical performance with an emotional sincerity that speaks directly to the heart."

I wanted to hug him, but I didn't dare move. So I just gazed at him, basking in his approval.

He smiled. "If you can develop your physical technique to match your dramatic instincts you'll have an outstanding career ahead of you."

Could I be dreaming? Was it possible I was standing face to face with the world-famous composer Antonio Vivaldi and he was saying these things to me?

"So now we'll begin your technical training in earnest." He moved from the harpsichord, picked up his violin, and played a short phrase. "Repeat that on 'ah'."

I did as he said, and he listened closely. He played the phrase again. "Now on 'eeh'." We went through all the vowel sounds. "Again." He started to repeat the exercise a half-tone higher.

After I'd sung the exercise several times, on higher

and higher tones, I felt tired and my shoulders sagged.

"Don't let your breath support collapse." He wrinkled his brow and without missing a beat continued up another semi-tone.

I squared my shoulders and breathed deeply.

Then, "Your throat is closing. Let your jaw hang loose, and *relax*." He went on with the exercise, driving me to higher and higher pitch levels. When I thought my head would burst if he made me sing any higher, he stopped, lowered the violin from his shoulder, and gave me an exasperated look. "You have a long way to go with your technique."

He was very worked up, and I wasn't sure if he was angry with me or just anxious for me to succeed.

I looked up at him, uncertainly. "I'm sorry."

"What's there to be sorry for? You simply must work, that's all. Talent will only get you so far. Musical perfection requires years of unrelenting practice. If you're willing to commit yourself to that, I'm willing to work with you." His encouraging smiles of just a few minutes before were gone. Now he looked intense and serious.

"I'm willing," I said, trying to sound more confident than I felt.

He gazed at me, frowning, then his mouth relaxed into a smile. "Annina," he said, sounding much calmer than he had a moment ago, "I don't want you to feel discouraged. You have instinctive abilities that'll serve you well in operatic performance, and I want to help you develop those abilities."

I felt encouraged enough to speak my mind. "I like to sing what I feel. And I want to make other people feel those things too."

"You certainly have the capacity to do that. But you'll make things more difficult for yourself if you disregard technique."

My heart dipped, and my defensive wall sprang into place. I lifted my chin. "You mean you want me to sound like Chiara."

"No, I definitely don't want that."

"Because she was your favorite prima donna?"

"Is that what she told you?"

"Everyone says so."

"Well, that shows how wrong people can be. Oh, Chiara warbles well enough, but her style is purely ornamental. There's no fire fueling her singing or igniting her passions. She's cold as ice."

I was dumbstruck, amazed at his bluntness. For weeks I'd heard nothing but praise for Chiara's brilliant mastery of singing technique. And now Don Antonio had negated all that with his curt assessment of her vocal style.

"Technique is artificial, he said, "something learned and cultivated. But it must be mastered all the same if you're to acquire the tools necessary to fully express those violent inner passions of yours."

I felt myself blush.

Concern and amusement mingled in his smile. "What you feel in your heart, Annina, can't be taught. It's part of you, and no one has the right to try to take that from you. If your talent doesn't match so-called conventional standards, so much the better, I say."

My sinking heart swelled. To have the chance to sing onstage, sure of my voice, would be the answer to all my prayers and the fulfillment of my long-held dream.

Yet I wondered how my singing could ever compete with those dazzling voices I'd heard at the opera—voices trained to the height of technical brilliance. I wanted to tell Don Antonio my fears and be comforted by his reassurance.

I hid that desire. I wasn't ready to expose that much of myself to him.

CHAPTER 10

La Morte

Death

My lessons with Don Antonio were a fierce ritual of emotional highs and lows. His unpredictable mood swings and constant energy kept me on my toes, but also tormented me with uncertainty. One minute he'd scold me for a lapse in technique and the next he'd praise me for my dramatic expressiveness. As his look shifted from a dark, furrowed brow to a sunny smile, he took me from the depths of despair to the heights of happiness. In some ways he frightened me. Yet I found myself growing more attached to him as the weeks went by.

My growing attachment to Don Antonio led me to trust him more and more. Still, Chiara's threats about the letter gnawed at me. I wanted so much to confide in him and tell him everything she'd put me through, but I was too afraid she'd show him the letter.

Then one day it struck me that maybe I could ask Don Antonio to send a message to the duke. They were friends, I assumed, and probably kept in touch. If the letter wasn't mailed from Signora's house there'd be no way Chiara could snatch it.

That night I scrawled a quick note to the duke, explaining how trapped I felt. I was sure he'd be able to use his influence to weaken Chiara's hold over me. I didn't plan to tell Don Antonio anything about what I wrote in the letter, but I'd ask him at my lesson the next day if he'd mind sending it. Surely he'd do that for me.

The following afternoon I rushed back to my room after dinner to fetch the letter, which I'd hidden in my satchel under the bed. As I tore through the limp satchel, panic crept through me. The letter had disappeared.

Unnerved, I looked up to see Chiara at the door.

"You think your noble duke and your adoring maestro will rescue you from your troubles? Think again."

I silently raged at myself for being stupid enough to give Chiara yet another chance to blackmail me with her snooping.

"What do you mean?" I said.

"My father could buy them both out in a heartbeat. And he'll do it if I ask him to."

"But why would he—why would you—want to do

that?"

"I have my reasons. Just consider yourself warned."

A few hours later I arrived at Don Antonio's studio, and it was as if a dark cloud hovered over the room. Chiara stood with her arms crossed, frowning, and Don Antonio seemed to be searching for something. I watched with dread as she pulled him aside and whispered to him. They both glanced at me, and my knees went weak.

Chiara pointed to me. "That girl has ruined the manuscript to one of your motets. Yes, the botched copy she made is here, but the original is nowhere to be found. I'm sure she stole it to hide the evidence. I was going to give it back to you, maestro, but now it's gone."

I was stunned and mortified. I'd returned that manuscript to her in perfect condition weeks ago, and now she was making up a lie to cause me more trouble. No doubt she'd hidden the score herself. But I was defenseless. As long as she had my letters I couldn't dare say anything to cross her.

"It's really not that important, Chiara," Don Antonio said. "Please excuse us now, so Annina and I can get on with our lesson."

Chiara glared at me, then flounced out of the room in a flurry of anger. The dark cloud passed, and things started to feel all right again. Still, my fear of Chiara was driving me to be more cautious—and defiant.

I even went on the defensive with Don Antonio. "So

it wasn't good enough?" I asked, when he seemed less than enthusiastic about the aria I'd just sung for him. I didn't mean to be peevish. But Chiara's relentless attacks were wearing me down.

He looked at me as if he could read my mind. "Annina, I know you're distressed about what happened here a few minutes ago. Chiara's behavior toward you is absolutely horrid. I'm beginning to understand what you've had to put up with since you came here, and I don't blame you for feeling upset and discouraged."

My eyes misted and I bit my lip to keep it from trembling. He put his arm around me for a moment, and I leaned my head against his shoulder, savoring the warmth of his closeness.

THE NEXT DAY was Saturday, and since I had no lesson I decided to visit the sewing room. I'd been relieved of my sewing duties when I started lessons with Don Antonio, but I still liked to spend time with Graziana.

"I heard he stuck up for you yesterday," she said, arching her eyebrows.

"What?"

"When Chiara tried to stir up trouble, jumping all over you about her silly motet."

"How do you know about that?"

"Because Chiara doesn't know when to keep her mouth shut." She narrowed her eyes and leaned closer to me. "Yesterday she came home all aflutter, carping on about how 'that irksome child' ruined her motet score and that Don Antonio refused to take her side against you. She even implied you have some kind of hold over him. She's terribly jealous, you know, of any female he takes an interest in, especially one as young and pretty as you. And when she's jealous she can be dangerous." She said all this in a rushed whisper, flitting her eyes toward the room's open door.

I didn't care about the open door. I was too interested in something Graziana had just said.

"You think I'm pretty?"

She raised her eyebrows. "Have you seen yourself in a mirror lately? You're more than pretty—you're gorgeous."

I'd never thought of myself as pretty, much less gorgeous. And Graziana wasn't one to flatter. I felt a rush of pleasure, but decided I'd better go back to the discussion about Chiara.

"I just don't understand why she hates me so much. It seems like she's trying harder than ever to ruin things for me."

"She feels threatened by you."

"*Why*? I've never said or done anything to threaten her."

"You didn't have to. She was already fuming that the duke dropped her in favor of you. And now she's gotten worse because she can't stand the special attention you get from Don Antonio. Ever since she first came to Venice she's been trying to wangle her way into his favor, and in her view you're a major hindrance."

"But now it seems she doesn't even like him."

"She doesn't. She's too self-centered to really like anyone. But she thinks she can manipulate him into getting her what she wants."

"Why does she want to manipulate him if her father's so rich and powerful?"

Graziana looked at me with an ironic little twist at the corner of her mouth. "Like I've told you before, Chiara fantasized for years that her 'rich and powerful' father would use his money and influence to launch her into the brilliant opera career she's always dreamed of. But her brag that he'll do anything she asks is all bravado. He's never even acknowledged her. So to make up for it she keeps trying to use her beauty and charm to latch onto powerful men and exploit them for her selfish purposes. But they all get disenchanted with her sooner or later."

"The things you've told me about Chiara almost make me feel sorry for her," I said, frowning.

Graziana rolled her eyes. "Don't waste your pity on her, Annina. She's brought it all on herself. And she's a snaky one, so I'd watch my step if I were you."

An uneasy feeling slithered through me. I hesitated a moment, then said quietly, "Chiara stole a very private letter I wrote my sister. There're secrets in that letter that must never get out."

She looked worried. "You have to get it back from her, Annina. There's no telling what she'll do with information like that. At the very least she'll use it to blackmail you and control you completely."

"She's already doing that," I said, in a shaky whisper. "How can I possibly get it back from her?" I was frantic now. Graziana had spelled out plainly the shadowy dread I'd been feeling.

"Don't worry, Annina." Her calm voice was reassuring. "I'll think of something. You'll get your letter back."

EARLY THE NEXT MORNING I crept downstairs before church to talk to Graziana about the letter problem. Fiametta, Marzia, and Ernesta were crowded in the hallway outside her room, whispering among themselves. I managed to catch bits and pieces of what they said. "Have you heard? . . . I've heard something, but I'm not sure . . . I think it was something she ate . . . will she be all right? . . . poor Graziana!"

A knot formed in my stomach. "What's going on?" I asked Fiametta.

She gave me a wry look, as if she were deciding if she should let me in on their secret. "Graziana became very ill quite suddenly last night," she finally said, in a shrill whisper.

"Ill? How ill? What's wrong with her?" The knot in my stomach tightened.

"Food poisoning, I think." She looked past me. "Here comes Signora with the doctor."

Signora hurried down the hall, looking more somber and worried than I'd ever seen her. I felt like I'd scream if somebody didn't tell me what was happening.

Then Chiara appeared. Every inch of her displayed a chilling calm.

Icicles slid up my spine. I closed my eyes and prayed silently. *Please, God, please. Not this. Graziana's my only friend. Don't take her away from me.*

Signora and the doctor went into Graziana's room while everyone else hovered outside the door. After what seemed like an eternity, they came back into the hall. The doctor's face looked grim. Signora dropped her head and tightened her mouth and eyes. They didn't have to tell me. I knew. *La morte!* Death! Graziana had died, and I was completely alone.

Time seemed to stand still. Dazed, I plodded back to my room and took *la moretta* out of the trunk. Sinking face-down into my pillow, I slipped her under the quilt. I tried to cry but couldn't. It was like my mother's abandonment all over again, only now Papà and Paolina weren't here to comfort me. I couldn't even write to them, because Chiara would steal my letter, and that would give her more leverage against me. I'd been silenced. My hands tightened into fists and I squeezed my pillow in excruciating frustration. When would this ever end?

I felt a presence standing over me. Flipping over, I propped on my elbow.

Chiara's cat-like green eyes stared into mine, and her mouth was fixed in a frigid half-smile. "So much for your cozy friendship," she said after an agonizing moment, her voice cutting through me like an ice-pick. "I hope you see now that you're totally under my power and no one can help you." Her sinister smile broadened into a fiendish grin.

I shrank from her in horror. She was using this tragedy to her own advantage, to make me feel hopeless. And there was nothing I could do about it. Looking into her cold eyes, I knew I was defeated. I sank back on my pillow, and Chiara left as abruptly as she'd appeared.

In dry-eyed misery I pulled *la moretta* from beneath the quilt and laid her on my face. *Shield me, protect me*, I begged silently.

Then I remembered that tomorrow was my birthday. But what difference did it make? I was growing older, yet more powerless, with each passing day.

CHAPTER 11

Il Compleanno

The Birthday

No one seemed to know it was my birthday. I was fifteen today, old for a debutant singer, and no closer to my dream of singing in the opera. My only friend was gone, and Chiara had turned more vicious than ever. I'd never felt so downhearted.

Just before dinner Chiara confronted me in her usual haughty way. I tried to walk past her.

"Not so fast," she said, grasping my arm. "I have plans for you. I want you to transcribe another motet I'm singing at church next Sunday."

I jerked my arm from her clutching hand. "No, I can't do that. Don Antonio told you I'm not a copyist."

"Well, he's not here, is he? So you'll do as I say." The

sharpness in her voice resonated with threatening overtones. She raised her chin. "Need I remind you that you're completely under my power?"

Her brazen tone was more than I could stomach. "I'm not in your power. Just because you say I am doesn't make it true. Do whatever you want to me, but I won't be your slave."

The edges around Chiara's mouth hardened, and her eyes blazed. "Don't forget I have your treasured letters and I won't hesitate to use them against you."

"I don't care a fig about those letters." I tried to sound offhanded but could barely control the tremor in my voice. "They're just the silly ramblings of a fourteen-year-old girl. Who'll care what they say?"

She glared at me for a long instant, the corners of her mouth twitching. Finally she said, "I think I'll show your *secret* letter to Don Antonio."

I forced myself to look calm. "Do you really think he'd be interested in a girl's frivolous writings? I'm sure he has more important things on his mind. If you pester him to read that nonsense he'll be more annoyed with you than he already is."

I braced myself for the onset of her fury.

But for the first time since I'd known her, Chiara was at a loss for words. She stared at me with wide, blinking eyes, and she tightened her mouth, as if to keep her lip from quivering. Part of me almost pitied her. But another part of me enjoyed watching her squirm.

"We'll see about that," she finally said, then turned on her heel and stalked off in a huff.

I felt better than I had in a long time. I was fifteen today and not a timid little girl anymore. I wasn't about to let Chiara keep me paralyzed with fear.

At dinner, Signora made her grand entrance as usual. But instead of her typical stony look, today she was smiling primly. When she reached her place at the head of the table, she gave the blessing, and remained standing.

"Ladies, I have an announcement to make."

Graziana is dead. My heart turned over and shriveled as the reality of it flooded my mind.

"As you know, our dear seamstress, Graziana, took ill the evening before last," Signora said. "She grew steadily worse during the night, and early yesterday morning the doctor said she would not live. But over the past few hours, praise be to God, she's shown marked improvement. The doctor examined her again a few moments ago and has informed me that Graziana is out of danger."

I was so ecstatic I almost fell out of my seat.

"YOU CERTAINLY LOOK HAPPY today," Don Antonio said, when I arrived at his studio that afternoon.

"I am, maestro, today's my birthday."

"Your birthday? Well, congratulations. How old are you now?"

"Fifteen." I felt giddy, anxious to share my happiness. "And the most wonderful thing has happened. My friend Graziana, who was so sick yesterday and almost died, is much better now. She's going to be all right."

"Graziana?"

"The seamstress who lives at Signora Malvolia's house. She's the only person, besides you, who's been nice to me since I've been here."

He looked at me in a very tender way. "Oh, I see. Well, I'm happy for your sake and for Graziana's of course, that she's out of danger."

"It's the best present I could have had."

His smile was warm. "I have another present for you, Annina."

"Really? What is it?"

"Do you remember Rosane's aria, *Solo quella guancia bella* from *La verità*, that you learned a few months ago?"

"Yes, I love that aria."

"I've rewritten it for you, with new words." The score he picked up from the harpsichord glistened with fresh ink. He held it out to me. "Now it's your very own aria."

I took the score eagerly and saw he'd renamed it "*La mia bella pastorella*." He'd even written "For Annina" at the top.

"*Grazie*, maestro!"

"Now let me tell you why I did this. I'm putting together a *pasticcio*, a staged performance of arias from several of my operas. It's to take place next month, in Treviso, a town just a little north of here. I'm calling it *La ninfa infelice e fortunata,* The sad and lucky nymph. I'd like you to play the part of a shepherd boy and sing this aria.

"You mean . . .you want me to sing in a public performance?"

"Well, considering your advancing age I'd say it's high time you made your stage debut," he said, his mouth curled in a slightly wry twist.

I wanted to throw my arms around him, but I wasn't sure how he'd feel about that. I'm fifteen now, I told myself. I need to learn to control my wild urges. So I just clasped my hands in a ladylike way and enveloped him in the radiance of my smile.

LATER THAT EVENING, alone in my bedroom, I ran my hands along the contours of my naked body. I was still very slender, but it seemed like, overnight, I'd started to develop a few curves in the right places. Passing my fingers over my swelling breasts, I felt a strange tingling deep inside.

I pulled on my nightgown, slipped into bed, and

wrapped my arms around the cool pillow. The tingling quickened. How fast things can change. Graziana had practically died and come back to life, I'd amazed myself by standing up to Chiara, and Don Antonio had paved the way for my opera debut. My fifteenth birthday had turned out to be quite a day. I wasn't a child anymore.

THE NEXT MORNING I visited Graziana.

"I'm so glad you're better now," I said, with a cheery smile. "I have lots to tell you."

"Well what's stopping you? Tell, tell!"

"I had a really good lesson with Don Antonio yesterday."

"Yes?"

"He's written a special aria for me, and he wants me to sing it in a show he's putting together in Treviso next month. I'm going to be a shepherd boy."

"How adorable. What will you wear?"

"Oh, I don't know. I haven't even thought about that."

"Leave it to me. *I'll* design and make your costume."

"Will you really? That'll be wonderful. Now you *have* to get better."

Signora appeared and ordered me out of the room.

As I said goodbye to Graziana, she pulled me close

and whispered in my ear. "I'd love to see the look on Chiara's face when she hears about this."

I stifled a giggle.

AT MY LESSON I told Don Antonio that Graziana had offered to design and make my costume. "Is that all right?" I asked.

"Yes, I suppose that's fine, if that's what you want."

Then he made me go over and over the technical exercises he'd given me to practice. He was so pleased by my progress, he decided to let me sing a second aria in the pasticcio, *Son come farfalletta*, I am like a little butterfly. And that's exactly how I felt—happy and lighthearted as a butterfly.

TO MY SURPRISE, and much to my relief, Chiara left me alone during the weeks leading up to my debut in Treviso. Whenever I saw her she acted as if I didn't exist. It worried me that she still had my letters, and I almost felt confident enough to say something to Don Antonio about it. But a murky fear stopped me. My debut loomed so close I could taste it, and I was afraid to do anything that could possibly ruin my big chance.

A FEW DAYS before the show, Graziana had my costume ready. She sent me into her dressing room, eager for me to try it on. The costume was very simple: a thin cotton tunic, with short, loose sleeves, in a dazzling shade of teal green, along with a brimless cap made of the same fabric. For my legs there were pale blue stockings, and for my waist a cloth belt. I slipped out of my dress and underclothes and into the strangely winsome little outfit.

The tunic was daringly short, reaching to just above my knees. My body felt so free it seemed like I was wearing almost nothing. I stuffed my hair into the cap, wrapped the belt around my waist, and came out to show Graziana.

With a weak smile, I said, "Um . . . Graziana, do you really think my legs should be so exposed on a public stage?"

"Why not? You have lovely, slender legs. If I had legs like yours I surely wouldn't miss a chance to show them off."

"How do you think Don Antonio will feel about this costume?"I asked, hoping she'd realize he'd find it shockingly improper.

"He'll love it."

"Won't he think it's a little indecent?"

"Of course not. He may be a priest, but he's no prude.

He's created a special role for you and he'll want you to look the part. You know better than anyone how much he values dramatic truth over stuffy decorum."

Over the next few days I grew more confident about the costume. It was sure to make quite an impression.

AT LAST THE BIG DAY ARRIVED. It was just after Easter, and Graziana and I, along with Don Antonio and his entourage of singers, instrumentalists, and stage technicians, set out early that morning. We reached the mainland by boat, and coaches carried us past countless stately patrician villas along the *Terraglio*, the highway to Treviso.

After a short rehearsal and dinner, Graziana went to work getting me dressed and made up. Then it was show time. The orchestra played the opening sinfonia, and the curtain went up. I waited anxiously backstage for my entrance, which was to come near the end of the first act.

Before I knew it, the aria before mine was ending, and Graziana rushed to my side. "This is it, Annina, you're on!"

I took a deep breath, stepped out of the wings, and walked to center stage. Don Antonio lifted his violin to start the orchestral introduction. My eyes caught his, and he gave me an encouraging smile. My heart swelled with excitement.

Then I saw Chiara sitting near the front of the pit. Her eyes were fixed on me with the smug sureness that I was about to make a fool of myself. My confidence collapsed, and my swelling heart turned to stone.

CHAPTER 12

Il Debutto

The Debut

Don Antonio led the violins in an introduction that sounded like the graceful fluttering of little butterfly wings. I felt like those butterflies were flapping frantically in my stomach. As the flittering notes of the orchestral prelude darted toward my opening phrase, a viselike grip tightened around my jaw, throat, and chest.

My vocal entrance was only a few beats away, and I couldn't even get enough air in to sing a note. At best I might manage a shrill screech, which would send the audience into gushes of laughter and jeers. My mind filled with the stories Mamma used to tell me about the rotten fruit and tomatoes peevish spectators hurled like missiles when they were dissatisfied with a singer's performance. I wanted to run from the stage to the safety of the shady wings. But my feet felt frozen to the stage floor, and my legs shook with so much violence I was afraid if I tried to move I'd fall on my face. Why did Graziana have to design a costume that exposed my trembling knees to everyone?

The introduction seemed like it would never end. Then, just one more beat before my ultimate humiliation and the end of my career and my dreams—and, I was sure, the end of my association with Don Antonio. He'd despise me now, or worse, pity me.

Gasping what little air I could, I glanced at him in desperation. Surely he knew me well enough by now to sense my terror. And surely he'd frown in disgust at my cowardice. But he didn't frown. He didn't smile either, yet his deep blue eyes shone into mine in a way that somehow fueled my determination to get through this. I lifted my head and plunged into the aria.

At once my fear vanished, and in its place came a warm surge of confidence. I was no longer powerless, downtrodden Annina. I was a sprightly, carefree shepherd boy comparing myself to a butterfly.

I am like a little butterfly
that in the middle of two lights
ventures here and there.

The aria's lively rhythm filled me with energy. My voice flowed easily, and I sang with an exhilarating sense of joy. All too soon it was over, and the audience exploded with applause.

Backstage, I ran into Graziana's arms.

"*I've never heard such tantalizing singing!*" The orchestra had already started the introduction to the next aria, so she spoke in a hushed tone. "And I must say the costume I designed for you shows off your character to absolute perfection."

"You're right," I said, trying to catch my breath. "As soon as I started singing I knew the costume was perfect. It really helps me feel the part I'm playing. But Graziana, I almost thought I wouldn't be able to do it. Just before I started to sing I saw Chiara in the front row, and I was suddenly scared to death."

"I was afraid of that," she said with a sigh.

"You knew she was here? How did she get here?"

"I didn't tell you this before because I didn't want to ruin things for you. But when Chiara found out Don Antonio was taking you to Treviso for your opera debut she nearly went insane with envy. She badgered Signora until the old crone agreed to arrange transportation for her. You know what though? I'm glad Miss High and Mighty came. I'm glad she's seeing with her own eyes and hearing with her own ears how talented you are. Now she really has something to stew about."

I grinned and nodded. I felt much more relaxed now, and the rest of the performance seemed to whiz by. Between acts, Graziana took me to the dressing room to fuss with my makeup and costume. Soon it was time for my second aria, *La mia bella pastorella*, in which I sang of my love for a beautiful shepherdess.

At the end of the final act the singers came out one by one to bask in the audience's applause. Since I was the youngest, and had one of the smallest parts, I came out first. The audience went wild, clapping, cheering, stomping, and throwing flowers. Don Antonio gazed up at me, his face glowing with triumph and delight. Flushed with joy, I capered off the stage amid cries of "*Brava la bella Annina! La piccola Mantovanna, Bravissima!*"

I ripped off the little shepherd's cap, and my hair tumbled around my shoulders. Graziana rushed over and hugged me.

"Did you hear what they were saying, Graziana? They called me 'beautiful Annina, the little girl from Mantua'!"

She grinned with pride. "I did indeed. Annina, you were brilliant!"

Graziana's eyes darted past me, and her smile hardened into a frown. I turned and saw Chiara. Her face, darkened by fury, contrasted eerily with the intricate coils of her icy blond hair. Without a word she shot me a cutting glare and swept past me.

"You might as well get used to it," Graziana said, sighing. "Opera singers are known for their haughty ways and endless intrigues."

But I was too elated to worry about Chiara's intrigues.

I was still giddy with happiness when Don Antonio came backstage after the final curtain call.

"*Bravissima*, Annina! You were superb. You completely enraptured the audience. Even I couldn't have imagined how beautifully you'd sparkle and bring your character to life onstage."

I quivered with pleasure. Then I was startled by a vaguely familiar voice.

"Very well said, maestro. I couldn't have said it better myself."

I looked behind me and was stunned to see the duke. "Your Excellency!" I squeaked. Flustered, I tripped over my awkward curtsy, but Don Antonio caught my elbow. My face went hot with embarrassment.

The duke exuded easy charm as he looked me over. "How you've grown, Signorina Annina. You are indeed a vision of loveliness."

His exaggerated grin and the hard gleam in his eye made me cringe with self-consciousness. I was glad Don Antonio was there, and without even thinking I stepped closer to him.

"Maestro, you're to be commended for accomplishing such wonders with this enchanting young lady."

Don Antonio didn't seem impressed by the duke's

oozing flatter. "The credit goes entirely to Signorina Girò, Excellency."

The duke's grin became roguish, and he responded slyly. "Come now, maestro, you are much too modest."

But his eyes were on me. He started to move in my direction, and I smelled brandy on him.

Don Antonio glared at him, unsmiling, then turned his attention to me. "You'd better change, Annina, before you catch a chill."

"*Sì*, maestro." How grateful I was he'd given me a means of escape. I bobbed another curtsy and said, "So nice to see you again, Excellency," before I scurried off.

When I reached the stairs leading to the dressing rooms I glanced back and saw that Don Antonio and the duke were still talking. But I was out of earshot and had no idea what they were saying.

Graziana was waiting for me in the hall outside the large dressing room I was sharing with several other female singers.

"Annina, there you are. Where've you been? It's chilly in here, and you're going to catch your death if you don't put something on."

"I know, Don Antonio just said the same thing."

"Well, he's certainly looking out for you, isn't he?" Graziana's lips curled, and her eyes brightened. "Isn't this wonderful? Chiara's going to go mad with envy, if she hasn't already."

I tried to smile, but an uneasy feeling had crept over me.

She crinkled her brow. "What's wrong? You seem worried about something."

"It's nothing, really."

"Well it must be *something*. You were so happy just a few minutes ago."

I sighed. "It's just that the duke suddenly showed up when I was talking to Don Antonio. He looked at me in a strange way that was kind of scary."

Graziana smiled in her easygoing way. "Oh good heavens, Annina, you know how men are. You look adorable in that charming little costume, and you can't blame them for noticing. Don't even give it another thought," she said, waving her hand past her face.

I still found the duke's unexpected appearance unsettling. It wasn't just his leering that bothered me. Seeing him again reminded me of the first time I'd met him, at Papà's shop, and the memory of that day caused the reality of my family's troubles to agitate my heart anew.

These thoughts were still flowing through my head back at Signora Malvolia's house. I remembered how old, sad, and helpless Papà looked the last time I saw him. A sudden fear gripped me. What if he got sick? What if he *died*? What if I never saw him again?

I thought about Chiara's shameless harassment and seethed with anger. Worst of all, she'd cut me off from my family. Well that'll change tomorrow, I decided, with a burst of conviction. I'll confront her and find a way to *make* her stop stealing my mail.

But how would I do it? Graziana had offered again to intervene for me, but I'd assured her I could handle the problem myself, though I had no idea how. I considered speaking to Don Antonio about the letters, then decided against it. I can't expect him to solve all my problems for me, I told myself. If I don't stand up to Chiara on my own I'll never be free of her bullying.

THE MORNING AFTER my return from Treviso, Ernesta approached me in her usual curt way. "Signora wishes to see you in her study immediately."

Dio mio. What have I done now?

CHAPTER 13

L'Impazienza

Impatience

Signora sat at her desk, reading glasses perched on her nose, and her mouth set in a hard frown.

"You wished to see me, Signora?"

"Be seated, Annina. I have a question to ask you." Her voice and manner were as dry as dust, but I noticed the knuckles of her bony fingers had gone white from clutching a small bundle of papers.

"Yes, Signora?" My insides churned. Her chilling attitude could only mean I was in serious trouble.

"I would like you to tell me the whereabouts of Chiara."

"I don't know what you mean, Signora."

"I find that hard to believe. Several days ago, against my better judgment, I granted you permission to accompany Don Antonio to Treviso for a theater performance. I was against it, but the maestro was quite insistent, and he is a difficult man to say no to."

In spite of my fear, I had to suppress a smile.

Signora took off her glasses, cleared her throat, and drew herself into a rod-like posture. "After you left, Chiara informed me that Don Antonio had requested her presence in Treviso as well."

I was sure this wasn't true, but I held my tongue.

"I found it quite odd that Don Antonio hadn't mentioned that to me. But, of course, I had no reason to doubt Chiara's word."

Of course not, was my ironic thought.

"So I hired a private coach in order that she might travel to Treviso in a manner befitting her station."

It almost seemed like Signora was trying to justify to me, or perhaps to herself, how she'd been duped by Chiara.

"Yesterday I received word that she was missing." Signora paused, as if for dramatic effect.

On pins and needles, I waited for her to go on.

"I would like you to tell me where she is."

"I'm sorry, Signora, but I have no idea."

"Surely you must have known she was there."

"Yes, I saw her for only a minute. But we didn't speak to each other."

"Perhaps Don Antonio knows where she is," she said, with a sly tinge to her voice.

The corners of my mouth tightened. "That I wouldn't know, Signora."

She pursed her lips. "You and he have become quite close, haven't you?"

"I'm not sure I know what you mean, Signora," I said, shifting in my chair.

"I mean it's been noted that you spend a great deal of time at his studio."

I started to feel vaguely indignant. "I'm taking singing lessons with him, as you know, and lately there's been a lot to do to get ready for the performance in Treviso."

"Has there, now?" Signora's mouth and jowls angled down, and she leaned toward me in a threatening way.

I caught my breath.

"I want you to listen to me carefully, Annina. You are to tell me immediately what Don Antonio knows about Chiara's disappearance."

I felt tightness in my chest and jaw but forced myself to meet her frowning gaze. "If you want my opinion, Signora, I don't think he knows anything about it. But if you don't believe me, why not ask him yourself?" I hoped she would. He'd set the old battleaxe straight.

Signora's mouth became a pinched line, and her white-knuckled fists shook. "I am incensed at your audacity, Annina! How. . . how *dare* you presume to give me orders concerning Don Antonio, to . . . to speak to me in that way!"

I looked at her dried-up, quivering face and realized she was afraid of him. Even though Don Antonio was warm and friendly most of the time, I'd seen how intimidating he could be when overbearing people tried his patience. And Signora could certainly do that.

But it wouldn't do me any good to get any more on her bad side than I already was. I decided I should humble myself a bit to appease her. "Please forgive me, Signora. I didn't mean any disrespect." Then I thought I'd better add, "And I certainly hope no harm has come to Chiara."

Signora simpered. "Indeed, we must pray to God that she's safe." Her eyes misted, and her voice took on a nostalgic tone. "Oh, I'll never forget the day that darling girl first came here. She has been like a daughter to me ever since. Yes, she's always exhibited beauty, charm, and grace. Who could not love and admire her?"

I tried to look wistful, but I felt like retching.

"And so gloriously talented! Her voice is like that of an angel." All of a sudden Signora snapped out of her sentimental mood. She squared her shoulders and glared at me in an accusing way. "Why, she was Don Antonio's favorite—that is, until *you* came along. Since you've been his student he's lost interest in her."

There was a tense silence. She seemed to be waiting for my reaction. I couldn't think how to respond, so I just gazed back at her with what I imagined to be a perplexed look.

She eyed me shrewdly. "It intrigues me, Annina, how at times you are such an open book about your emotions, yet at other times, when I would expect a revealing reaction from you, your feelings are quite unreadable."

I sighed silently and started to fidget. The conversation had become tedious, and I was anxious to escape Signora's stifling presence. But she seemed determined to stare me down till I responded to her ridiculous implication.

"I'm sorry, Signora, but I really don't know what to say."

"Then perhaps you'll have something to say about *these*." She shoved the bundle of folded papers she'd been clutching at me.

I looked down and gasped.

"In the hope of finding some clue to Chiara's whereabouts, I searched her room last night. I found this stack of *your* correspondence—some written by you, and some written to you—among her things. I'd like you to explain how these letters got there."

I bit my lip and tried hard to steady my breathing. If I was to have any chance of walking out of that room with my mail I'd have to guard my tongue. I took a deep breath and looked her in the eye. "Very soon after I arrived here, Chiara told me she had the right to intercept my mail."

Signora stared at me, blinking. She opened her mouth as if to say something, then closed it. Finally she said, "Do you mean to say that you have had no communication with your family since you've been in Venice?"

"No, Signora, I haven't."

"Can you tell me Chiara's reason for doing this?"

I hesitated. "I can't say for sure, Signora."

She seemed to remember herself, and her tone grew sterner. "Are you aware of the seriousness of your accusation?"

"Yes, Signora."

"I see." She paused and looked at the bundle she still held in her hands. "Perhaps I should hold on to these letters myself, until I can learn Chiara's reason for confiscating them."

I had to think fast. I clasped my hands in my lap and spoke softly. "I humbly ask your permission to read the letters from my family, Signora. It troubles me deeply that I've had no contact with them since I've been here." Stinging moisture prickled my eyes.

Signora's face had returned to its typical iciness, but I thought I caught a glint of sympathy in her glance.

She stared at me for a long moment. "Very well, Annina," she finally said. "I suppose there can be no harm in allowing you to read these letters and correspond with your family. But be aware that I'll be watching you closely. Your unwillingness to share information with me about Chiara's disappearance gives me cause to question your integrity."

I was too overjoyed to be ruffled by her insult. "I'm so sorry I've caused you to feel that way, Signora. But I promise if I think of anything that might help you find Chiara, I won't hesitate to let you know."

WHAT A RELIEF to at last be freed from the prying questions of that pompous old windbag! It was almost dinnertime, but I rushed to my room to tear into the stack of letters. Since everyone was on their way to the midday meal I could read without interruption. I passed Ernesta in the hall and asked her to tell Signora I had a headache, so I wouldn't be joining the household for dinner.

Alone and trembling, I sat cross-legged on my cot with my pile of mail. The first letter was from Papà. As soon as I saw his handwriting my eyes clouded, and I had to keep dabbing them with a handkerchief to see clearly enough to read.

My Dearest Annina,

God alone knows how much I miss your lively presence. I think about you constantly, my little one, and pray that you are happy and well. Blessed as we are by His Excellency's kind generosity to you, I still wonder if sending you to Venice was the right thing to do. I worry much about you, my dear Annina, being so far from your loved ones. Perhaps I worry too much.

Your sister arrived home safely yesterday. She and I are well, though we still haven't heard from your mother. But I don't want you to worry yourself about that. She'll come back to us in good time, surely.

Please write to me soon, my little love, so I'll know you are safe and in good spirits.

Your Loving Papà
15 January 1722

I clutched the letter to my breast and leaned against the wall, weeping. Poor Papà. He must be frantic with worry, if he still wonders about me at all after so many months. With tear-drenched eyes I glanced again at the letter. Paolina had added a short note at the end:

Darling Annina, since I left you in the hands of that dreadful woman I haven't been able to think of anything else! Please write as soon as you can to let me know you are all right. In the meantime, I pray that someone kind will take you under their wing and protect you. It pains me more than I can say to think you might be treated harshly. I was very uneasy about leaving you in Venice, and I regret that my anxiety made me seem impatient with you. You deserve only love and tenderness, my sweet little sister.

Your Devoted Paolina

Oh, my dear Paolina. What I wouldn't give right now to have you here fussing over me. I sifted through the stack of mail and was relieved to find the "secret letter" Chiara had been using to blackmail me. Looking for more recent letters from home, I came across one from Paolina, postmarked the month before:

Dearest Annina,

Today is your 15th birthday, and Papà and I continue to be dismayed that we've heard nothing from you. If it were possible to come there myself and find out the cause of your silence, I wouldn't hesitate to do so. But Papà hasn't been well, and I cannot leave him.

I've sent several letters to Signora Malvolia inquiring about you, but they've all been returned unopened. The reason why is a complete mystery to me. And since I've received no letters from you, I can only imagine that, for some reason, you're being prevented from sending mail. This is quite bewildering.

Since none of the letters I've sent to you have come back, I can only pray that you've received and read them, and that you know how very much you are missed and loved.

Wishing you the Happiest
and most Blessed of Birthdays,
Paolina

I collapsed on my pillow, and my whole body shook with sobs. My tears of anguish over my loved ones were mixed with tears of rage at Chiara. How *dare* she cause my family such torment! All the letters' seals had been broken, so she must have read them and known the worry and heartache she was causing. How could anyone be so cruel?

I couldn't bring myself to re-read the agonized letters I'd written to Papà and Paolina during my first month here. And I decided they would never read them either. I didn't want them to ever know how much I'd suffered before Don Antonio came back to Venice. I smiled through my tears as I realized he must have been the answer to Paolina's prayer that someone kind would take me under their wing.

I'll write to Papà and Paolina and tell them about the wonderful things that have happened these past few months, I decided. But first I wanted to destroy all my old letters to them. I gathered the letters and crept quietly downstairs to the kitchen. Bettina was serving in the dining room, so I had the kitchen to myself for a few moments.

I took the letters to the hearth, threw them in, and watched them go up in flames. What an appropriate end for the last reminders of that nightmarish period of my life!

Just as quietly, I went back to my room and rummaged through my trunk for stationary and stamps. My eyes fell on *la moretta*, but I didn't touch her. "I have to do this myself," I told her. "I don't need your smothering protection."

I took out my writing board and started my letter:

My Very Dearest and Most Adored Papà and Sister,

This is the first chance I've had to write to you since I've been in Venice. Incredible as it might seem, my routine is so busy it's difficult to find time to write letters. I realize this negligence on my part is inexcusable, and I'm so sorry for the worry I've caused you. But I want you to know I'm happy and well.

So many things have happened since I've been here that it's hard to know where to begin. The very best thing is that I was fortunate enough to be accepted by Don Antonio as a private student. My studies with him have been very successful so far. And just two days ago I was allowed to go with him to Treviso to sing in a staged performance.

Papà, I don't want you to be distressed about this. It's what I sincerely want, and what makes me happier than anything in the world. Don Antonio is so kind, and a truly brilliant teacher. He's told me there's real potential in my singing, and I think he wants to do everything he can to help me.

Paolina, thank you for your birthday wishes. My 15th birthday was one of the best days of my life, and I'm sure your prayers helped make it that way.

I miss you both terribly and love you so much. I promise to write again soon.

All My Love,
Annina

Luckily it was post day, so my letter would be on its way to Mantua that very afternoon.

AT MY LESSON the next day, the first since Treviso, I didn't say anything to Don Antonio about Chiara's disappearance or the letters. I was too anxious to talk about my triumphant debut.

"So what did you think of my singing, maestro? Was I really all right?"

"You were marvelous."

I could hardly keep from bouncing up and down with joy. "Does that mean I can make my Venetian debut soon?"

"You need a lot more study before you'll be ready for that."

"But why? You just said I was marvelous."

"A Venetian opera performance is quite a different thing from a little *pasticcio* in a small town. Venice is the operatic center of the world, and audiences here expect singers to be top notch. Your time for that will come. In the meantime you must concentrate on perfecting your technique. *Ci vuol pazienza,* Annina."

I know it takes patience, I grumbled to myself. But my eagerness to sing again onstage threatened to overcome my better judgment.

CHAPTER 14

Il Teatro San Moisè

The Saint Moisè Theater

I was in my room getting ready for supper when I heard a quivering cry from below, as if someone just had the fright of her life. I rushed downstairs and saw everyone gathered in the front hall. Signora's hands were clasped to her heart and her eyes were as round as saucers. Chiara was at the door, bags in hand.

She stepped into the hall with an imperious air, while Signora babbled anxiously.

"Oh my dear! My darling! Where on earth have you been? I've been out of my mind with worry. Have we done something to vex you, my dear one? Oh please, *please* tell me what has distressed you so, that you would stay away for so many weeks!"

Chiara pushed past her with a terse reply. "A sudden opportunity came up. I didn't have time to tell you."

"Opportunity?" Signora's eyes widened all the more. "Oh, tell us about it, dear."

Chiara stopped and turned to us. "If you must know, I accompanied the Duke of Massa Carrara to Pesaro, where he arranged for me to star in two operas." She paused for an instant and gave me a chilling glance before heading for the stairs. Signora was close behind, stumbling over the hem of her gown.

During the next few weeks, even though Chiara continued to use Signora's house as her home base, she was away quite a bit without explanation. Signora wrung her hands with worry every time Chiara failed to come home at night, but on her return Chiara would turn a deaf ear to Signora's anxious questioning. None of this bothered me too much, since Chiara had apparently given up trying to torment me. I was perfectly happy to be left alone to focus on my studies with Don Antonio.

But early in May Don Antonio told me he would soon be going back to Rome, where he'd been commissioned to compose and direct sacred music for the holy feasts of Ascension and Pentecost.

I dreaded being left behind. Then an idea came to me. I'll ask him to take me to Rome with him. He took me to Treviso, why not to Rome? I could sing at the Vatican!

We had another lesson scheduled before he was to

leave, and I all but skipped into his studio. "*Salve*, maestro!"

He looked up from his desk, smiling. "Well, hello, Annina. What puts you in such good spirits?"

"I've just had a wonderful idea."

"Oh? What's that?" He'd turned his attention back to the score he was working on but kept smiling with interest at what I had to say.

"I'll go to Rome with you. Maybe I could even sing for the Pope." A jubilant grin spread across my face.

His eyes returned to mine. "I'm afraid that won't be possible."

"But *why*? You said I was splendid in Treviso. And you haven't let me sing in another performance since."

"You *were* splendid. But Treviso was a lucky opportunity, a chance to test your skills in a safe setting. You're still much too inexperienced to face a less forgiving audience. And as for going with me to Rome, that's out of the question. There'd be no one to look after you there. Over the holy days the city will be swarming with pilgrims, not to mention all sorts of riffraff. Not a safe environment for a young girl."

"But I'd be with you."

He put down his pen and sighed. "What do you think I am, a nursemaid? That I'll have nothing to do in Rome but watch over you every minute? Be serious, Annina."

My eyes smarted and my chest felt tight. "I don't need

a nursemaid, and I don't need to be watched over every minute. I can take care of myself."

"Is that so?" The corners of his mouth curled ever so slightly, and he gazed at me for a moment, his eyes shining. Then he got up from his desk and walked to the credenza. "The best thing for you to do while I'm in Rome would be to go home to Mantua and spend time with your family." He started leafing through a score, as if to end the discussion.

"Why can't I sing in Rome?" I persisted.

He didn't look at me, but stared at the score, his brow furrowed. "Women aren't permitted to sing in church or onstage in Rome."

"What? That's not fair."

"Maybe not, but neither you nor I make the laws in Rome. His Holiness does, and we must respect that." His eyes met mine. "In any case, you're not ready for a debut in a major city. You're too young, and your voice is not yet developed enough to carry in a large church or theater without straining. Now please be reasonable, Annina, and do as I say. Go home to Mantua and rest your voice. When I return to Venice in a few weeks I'll send for you."

Don Antonio left for Rome the next day, and I wrote Paolina to let her know I'd be coming home for a long visit. Maybe it's for the best, I reasoned. I haven't seen my family or breathed the fresh air of the Mantuan countryside for over three months. Graziana had left to visit her mother in Padua for several weeks, so life would've been mighty lonely at Signora Malvolia's house. Yes, it would be good to go home.

TO MY ASTONISHMENT, Chiara approached me that evening with a friendly smile.

"Well Annina, what are you going to do with yourself all these weeks while Don Antonio's in Rome?" Her eyes sparkled, and for the first time I noticed charming dimples at the corners of her mouth.

"I'm going home to Mantua, to visit my family. I haven't seen them since I've been in Venice."

"Oh, what a shame. That you won't be here, I mean. I've just heard about a wonderful opportunity that would be perfect for you."

"What opportunity?" I asked, cautiously.

"My good friend, Signor Gaspari, has been appointed impresario at the Teatro San Moisè for the spring season. I'm singing principal roles in the four operas he's presenting. But one of the singers he hired to sing small parts in the operas has come down with a fever, and it seems she won't be well enough to perform at all. I told Gaspari I thought her roles would be perfect for your voice, and I think he'd be willing to let you try."

My heart started to race. *My Venetian opera debut.* I had

misgivings, though. "That sounds fabulous, Chiara, but I don't think Don Antonio would approve."

"Nonsense, Annina, you don't know him like I do. Believe me, he'll be pleased and proud. Just think how exciting it'll be to surprise him with the news of your triumph on a Venetian opera stage."

"I don't know . . ."

"How will you ever succeed in opera if you're afraid to take a risk? To have a career you must be willing to plunge in when you have the chance. And it's not as if you've never sung in public before. Why, you absolutely dazzled onstage in Treviso. The audience went mad for you. And everyone knows how fast you can learn new music. Even I've had to admit that." She pressed her palm to her chest and giggled, as if at her own foolishness. Then she reached over and grasped my shoulder. "You know you can do it. This is a golden opportunity, and you'd be crazy to turn it down."

She flashed me another winning smile, and I started to weaken. Then I had an uncomfortable thought. "Why are you suddenly being so nice to me? You've always told me I'll never make it as a singer."

"Oh, but you've proved me wrong. And I'm certainly willing to own up to my foolish error in judgment." She pouted. "I'm terribly sorry for all those times I was unkind to you. I'd like to make up for that by offering you my friendship. What do you say, Annina? Can we be friends?" She smiled and held out her hand to me. Her dimples almost glistened.

Chiara seemed sincere about making amends, and I decided it would be uncharitable not to meet her halfway. I took her hand.

Her smile glimmered. "That's the spirit. Don't you feel so much better now that we've buried the hatchet? *I* certainly do." She gave me a mock frown. "Now Annina, as your friend I insist you put these silly worries aside and come with me tomorrow to talk to Signor Gaspari."

I dashed off a quick note to Paolina, saying something had come up and I'd have to postpone my visit home.

THE FOLLOWING AFTERNOON Chiara and I took a gondola to the San Moisè.

"Oh, Tonio!" she said, waving, when we entered the spacious theater. Grasping my hand, she pulled me toward a heavyset man sitting at a harpsichord near the stage. "Here she is, the girl I was telling you about."

The man stood and looked me over appraisingly. "She's awfully scrawny, isn't she?"

I felt very uncomfortable under his critical gaze, like an object being scrutinized.

"Yes, it's true," Chiara said. "And I'm afraid her technique is a bit underdeveloped as well. But won't you give the poor girl a chance? She's quite a little actress."

Signor Gaspari's eyes narrowed. "How old are you, my girl?"

"Fifteen, sir."

He raised his eyebrows and ran his eyes over me again. "Fifteen? You look barely thirteen, and I don't have time to wet-nurse a neophyte."

My jaw tightened.

Chiara simpered. "Really, Tonio, how you exaggerate. Annina is far from a beginner. She's been studying for some time now—first with Maestro Tomaso Albinoni, and most recently with Don Antonio Vivaldi."

Signor Gaspari looked doubtful. "Does she have any experience?"

Chiara smiled cheerfully. "Oh yes. She sang splendidly last month in Treviso, in a *pasticcio* Don Antonio organized."

"Well, performing in a little *pasticcio* in Treviso is a far cry from singing an entire season on a Venetian opera stage. I don't think this is a good idea, Chiara."

"But, Tonio, I'm sure she'll do fine. Just wait till you see how she comes to life onstage. Don Antonio has said as much, and you know he never says anything he doesn't mean."

Signor Gaspari sighed and frowned down at me. "All right, all right. Let me hear you sing something." He picked up a score. "Sing this."

He sat at the harpsichord, and I faltered my way through the piece, my voice shaking. When I was finished he said nothing. He pressed his lips together and glared at Chiara.

Her smile almost glowed.

He looked at me again. "Can't you sing any louder than that?"

"I, um," I said, my knees quavering. "Don Antonio told me I'll strain my voice if I try to sing too loud."

He laughed. "Well let me tell you something, little miss. If you can't manage to generate more volume than that, you won't be heard beyond the footlights."

"Oh but she will," Chiara said. "I'll work with her. She's very nervous, poor thing. But she'll get over her fear, you'll see. I'll have her singing with strength and confidence in no time."

He stared at her a moment, then returned his gaze to me. "Does your teacher know about this, young lady?"

I bit my lip and looked at Chiara.

She spoke up quickly. "Don Antonio is in Rome and it would be difficult to reach him. But I'm certain he'd be pleased for his student to help us out in this time of need."

Signor Gaspari didn't look convinced, and unease crept through me.

Quite suddenly, though, he seemed to resign himself to the situation. "You're right, Chiara," he said, shrugging his shoulders and sighing. "It would be nearly impossible to find a more experienced singer to fill in for Rosa at this late date. I suppose we'll have to make do with this little mite."

"At last you're being sensible, Tonio." Chiara's eyes shone with triumph.

IT WAS OPENING NIGHT of Maestro Tomaso's *Loadice*, and I was singing the very small role of Clistene. I'd brought *la moretta* along in my satchel for good luck. But when it was time for my entrance I walked onstage with my heart thudding in my ears and my knees shaking so violently I thought I'd collapse.

I looked at the maestro's toad-like face behind the harpsichord. Remembering what Don Antonio had said about Maestro Tomaso's wife dying, I felt a flicker of pity for him.

I knew this wasn't right. Without Don Antonio's approval and support I felt dreadfully vulnerable. This was the terror and humiliation of performing in front of Maestro Tomaso's singing class a thousand times magnified. How could I have been foolish enough to think I could pull this off? I alternated between fear at what lay ahead and elation that I was making my Venetian stage debut. My dream was about to come true. But would that dream turn into a nightmare?

Somehow my voice became disembodied while I sang my one and only aria that night. My throat ached with the effort to get the sound out, yet it seemed like someone else was singing. I glanced toward Maestro Tomaso at one point and caught his eye. He looked older and more tired than ever, and his somber expression gave no clue what he was thinking.

By the time I finished my aria, the audience's curious looks had turned to angry grimaces and mocking sneers. The light applause and much louder catcalls while I was making my bows made me feel like I never wanted to sing onstage again.

CHAPTER 15

La Disperazione

Desperation

Back at Signora's house, I sobbed on Chiara's shoulder. "I was *awful.* Did you hear how they scoffed at me? I just can't go on. I can't sing the rest of the operas."

"There, there, darling," she said, stroking my hair. "You're being much too hard on yourself. It really wasn't as bad as you think. All you need to do is learn to project your voice a bit more, and you'll be fine."

"No, I can't. My throat already hurts from singing louder than I should. Tomorrow I'll tell Signor Gaspari he has to find somebody to replace me."

"But it's much too late to find anyone to replace you. You can't let everyone down by backing out now, dear. Don Antonio would be very displeased to hear you behaved so unprofessionally."

"He's going to be even more displeased when he finds out I sang these roles behind his back!" I choked on my last words as a new flood of tears welled up.

"Nonsense. Why on earth would he want to hold you back from the very thing he's been training you for? Your worries are for nothing, Annina darling."

I swallowed a gasping sob. "Are you sure, Chiara?"

"Of course I'm sure. You must think of tonight's performance as a learning experience. The first time is always the most difficult. Why, you should have heard *me* the first time I sang on a Venetian stage. But the worst is over now, and you're going to do much better next time. I'll help you. That's what friends are for, right, Annina?"

I nodded warily and wiped my eyes with the backs of my hands.

THE FINAL OPERA for San Moisè's spring season was *Il Nemico Amante*, The Hostile Lover. I had the part of Idalma, a bigger, more demanding role than my other three had been. Chiara had coached me for the part, encouraging me to sing with even more power than before and to push my voice as forcefully as I could. She assured me all singers had to do this to be heard over the orchestra.

I sang that night with all the passion and strength I could muster, but my voice felt so strained I was barely able to make it through my final aria. Surprisingly, though, the audience seemed much more enthusiastic about my performance than they had before. I must have awed them with my acting skills.

After the final curtain call, as the audience started to scatter and leave, I peeked out from the wings and saw a man walk up to Signor Gaspari. They exchanged a few pleasantries, and I realized the man was a journalist.

His loud voice sailed across the stage to the far dark corner where I stood. "I must comment on Signorina Girò's performance."

My ears perked up, and I hovered in the shadows.

"Seldom have I seen or heard such an unbridled emotional display onstage. There's something quite unsettling about her singing. She shows an appalling lack of mastery of vocal technique."

Gaspari shook his head and murmured something I couldn't hear, but his tone and expression told me he was equally dissatisfied with my performance. My heart plunged as I realized my rush to make my Venetian debut had caused my career to be over before it started.

The journalist went on. "Yet I must say, signore, that the girl's dramatic execution displays a crude power and vitality."

I snapped to attention and strained my ears.

"I suppose I should congratulate you," he said, slapping Signor Gaspari's shoulder with his large paw.

Gaspari looked taken aback but fixed his mouth into a tight smile.

"I admire your courage in allowing this little sprite to make her professional debut with your company," the journalist said. "If I wasn't required by tradition to confine my critical acclaim to singers of the utmost technical excellence, I wouldn't hesitate to offer my endorsement of Signorina Girò."

IN SPITE OF the journalist's encouraging words, my reviews were terrible.

Chiara was delighted. "Well, well, little Miss Prima Donna, what a disappointment. I never imagined you could sing so badly. You're a laughingstock. You'll never be able to appear on a Venetian stage again."

The sparkle had left her eyes, and the charming dimples had retreated behind the corners of her smirking mouth.

"Chiara, you tricked me," I rasped in a voice almost too hoarse to speak. "You pretended to be my friend and talked me into doing this, knowing all along I'd fail!" I felt my face crumple. "When Don Antonio comes back and hears about this he's going to be furious with me."

She sneered. "How you fool yourself, Annina darling. Do you really think he cares that much? That you're the most important thing in the world to him? Believe me, you're not. It's pathetic how you overestimate his concern for you and your stupid little problems." Her cold green eyes surveyed me, and the corners of her pert mouth curled. "Of course, you know this means he'll drop you as a student. He won't work with people he can't trust."

"Why should I believe anything you say, Chiara? *You're* the one who can't be trusted. I'll never trust you again. *Ever!*"

She responded with her most sparkling laugh as she drifted airily out my bedroom door.

I ripped *la moretta* from my satchel, which I'd thrown on the bed. "And you!" I said, my voice a rasping croak. "You've finally got what you want, haven't you? I have no voice! My voice will never be heard on a Venetian stage again!"

I collapsed face down across the bed, shaking with sobs.

THE NEXT DAY, Graziana returned from Padua to find me brooding in the parlor.

"Annina, what's wrong? How was your trip to Mantua?"

"I didn't go." I barely managed to gasp the words out.

"Why not? And what's wrong with your voice? You sound raspy as a sanding file."

"My plans changed."

"Really? Well tell me about it."

"I don't know what went wrong, Graziana. Things were going so well for a while, and now things just couldn't be worse."

"Annina, you must tell me what's happened."

"After Don Antonio left for Rome, Chiara talked me into staying in Venice to fill in at the San Moisè for a singer who'd gotten sick."

"Oh dear. You didn't actually do it, did you?"

I looked down, nodded, and tears blanketed my eyes. "And it all turned out awful. I don't know how I could've been so stupid. Now Don Antonio won't want to have anything more to do with me."

Graziana looked concerned but tried to comfort me. She took me in her arms and patted my shoulder. "Come now, I'm sure it can't be all that bad."

I buried my face in her neck. "He's going to hate me now. I just know it."

"Nonsense. He could never hate you."

"Oh, Graziana, why didn't he take me with him to Rome, like I wanted him to? Then none of this would have happened."

She took hold of my shoulders and looked into my

eyes. "How could he have done that, Annina? He wouldn't have had time to look after you. And remember this: Rome is the center of the Catholic world. Don Antonio's operating right under the Pope's nose there and is expected to act like a priest. How would it look for him to go about Rome and the Vatican with a beautiful young girl clinging to him?"

I glared at her and frowned. But I knew she was right. Faithful, wise Graziana. If only she'd been here when Chiara started tempting me with her empty promises.

I sighed, exasperated. "Why does Chiara keep torturing me? Why is she so determined to see me fail?"

"Because she imagines you're succeeding where *she* failed."

"What do you mean?"

"I might as well tell you. I recently heard a very interesting story about Chiara and Don Antonio, from one of the other singers who starred in *La verità in cimento*, Anna Maria Strada. She came to me for a dress fitting just before I left town."

"What did she tell you?"

"Well, as you know, Don Antonio helped Chiara get her start. He gave her roles in several of his operas. And she adored him. But unlike you, she was always more interested in herself and her own personal ambitions than in him or anyone else. It didn't take long for her pompous opinion of herself to completely take over her better judgment."

My eyes widened. "Go on."

"According to Signora Anna Maria, after all the applause on *La verità*'s opening night, Chiara was so full of herself she proposed to Don Antonio that he should leave the priesthood and marry her."

I gasped, and my hands flew to my mouth. "You can't be serious!"

"Apparently she bragged to the other singers that he was in love with her."

I felt an unpleasant jolt but pressed on with my questions. "Well, what happened?"

"He rebuffed her, of course, and she's been fuming ever since. In fact, according to Signora Anna Maria, Chiara was so outraged by his rejection she was determined to spite him in some way."

"How awful. What did she do?"

"Remember the nasty satire I told you about? The one written by that hack Marcello?"

I nodded anxiously.

"Once the pamphlet got around, the owners of the San Angelo lost their confidence in Don Antonio and he was forced to give up his management of the theater. Marcello and his toadies moved in, took over, and replaced Don Antonio's program with a slew of boring, old-fashioned operas. Then Chiara signed a contract with the new management to sing in all those operas. Can you imagine it, Annina? After everything Don Antonio had done for her?"

So those were the "five operas in a row" that had strained her voice so much she had to stop performing for a season. And she'd alienated Don Antonio in the process. Served her right. Only now she'd trapped me into sharing her fate.

"I can't imagine how she could turn her back on him like that," I said, bristling with mingled shame and contempt.

"Well here's the really interesting part. All this led to a falling out between Benedetto Marcello and his older brother Alessandro, who really *likes* Don Antonio and his music."

"So then what?"

"Alessandro Marcello wrote to Princess Borghese in Rome, recommending that she arrange for Don Antonio to produce his latest opera there."

"And did she?"

"Yes. Which put Chiara in a real stew. *Then* she fumed because he didn't beg her to break her contract with San Angelo and come with him."

My jaw dropped. This was unbelievable. So Chiara imagined herself a scorned woman. If it wasn't so shocking it would be laughable. But why was she taking it out on me?

"So . . . do you think this has anything to do with the

way Chiara's treated me?"

"I think it has everything to do with it."

"*Why?*"

"She feels threatened by you. She's seen how much Don Antonio likes you, and she can't stand to see him even look at another female. It makes her crazy."

"But that doesn't make sense. She'd already turned against him before I even came here."

"It backfired on her, and she's still smoldering," Graziana said, with a gleam in her eye. "Think about it this way. He's obviously done just fine without her, and now he's shifted his interest to you. That's enough to drive her over the edge and make her really deadly. Like I keep telling you, Annina, you have to watch your step with her."

Coldness crept through me. It was the cold truth of Chiara's words: *Of course, you know this means he'll drop you as a student. He won't work with people he can't trust.*

CHAPTER 16

Il Pericolo

Danger

Paolina forwarded a letter to me. It was from Don Antonio, telling me he'd be back in Venice by the first of June. As much as I dreaded it, I knew I had to face him.

The day after his return I managed to slip out of the house when no one was looking and hurry through the maze of dark *calli* that opened onto the Campo Santa Maria Formosa. I scurried across the square and along the Rio del Mondo Novo until I reached the Vivaldis' house, at the Ponte del Paradiso. I knocked at the door, my stomach twisting with fear.

Margarita looked surprised to see me. She was gracious as always, but her smile seemed fixed. That wasn't a good sign.

When I entered the maestro's studio he was sitting at his desk. Eyeglasses rested on his arched nose, and he was frowning over a newspaper. More papers were scattered across his desk.

He looked up without smiling. "Hello, Annina."

There was a thud at the pit of my stomach, but I forced my lips into a tight smile. "*Salve*, Don Antonio. Welcome back."

He eyed me keenly. "I was surprised to learn you never left Venice."

"Well, um . . ." I tried to clear my scratchy throat. "Things didn't go like I'd expected."

"Yes, I can see that," he said, looking down again at the newspaper. "I asked Margarita to save all the Venetian opera reviews while I was away. It's a good thing she did, because I wouldn't have believed this if I hadn't seen it with my own eyes."

My skin turned to gooseflesh.

He took off his glasses and fixed his eyes on me. "How in the name of God did this come about, Annina? How could you consent to such a foolish thing, without my knowledge or approval?"

"I—the opportunity came about very suddenly. The singer who was supposed to do the parts got sick, and Signor Gaspari asked me to take her place."

He stared at me steadily. "I can't believe Gaspari would expect such a thing of you. There must be more to this than you're telling me."

My lip trembled, and my throat grew thick.

"Whatever the reason, this was absolutely foolhardy. You've damaged your voice, I could hear it the minute you opened your mouth. To think you could just breeze in and take over these roles, with no experience, no preparation—on a Venetian opera stage! You must have known I never would have allowed it. You weren't ready for this. I can't tell you how disappointed I am, Annina. I thought I could trust you."

I could think of nothing to say that seemed adequate. I started to crumble. My knees went weak and my heart beat wildly.

He went on. "If you'd followed my advice I would have soon been able to keep you employed with minor engagements that wouldn't tax your current capabilities, like I did in Treviso. Now you won't be able to make a public appearance in Venice for many more months, perhaps another year. Even if your voice recovers, audiences here have long memories, and you wouldn't be well received."

I stared at the floor, my cheeks flaming at his sharp words.

Finally I raised my eyes to his, emboldened by an urge to defend myself. "But I heard that newspaper man tell Signor Gaspari my singing has dramatic power."

"Then he's more astute than I would have thought."

He paused for a moment, and my body tensed as I waited to hear what he'd say next.

"But your admiring journalist also knows the current fashion doesn't value dramatic expression over technical brilliance. He certainly wouldn't put his career on the line by saying what he really thinks in print. And as for Gaspari, I can promise he'll never hire you again. He's far too cautious to risk going against his audiences' tastes."

His discouraging words made me feel hopeless. I pressed my lips together and blinked hard to hold back the hot tears gathering in my eyes.

He sighed, came around to the front of the desk and leaned against it, his arms folded. "I know you didn't bring this about yourself, Annina. Someone put you up to it. Who was it?"

I hung my head and twisted a handkerchief I'd pulled from my sash.

"Was it Chiara?"

My eyes filled, and I nodded without looking up.

He sighed again. I glanced at him timidly for an instant. His eyes were closed, and he was rubbing his forehead.

I looked down quickly, and he went on. "I should've known. May I ask how she managed to persuade you to go so completely against my wishes?"

I couldn't stop the silent tears that trickled down my face. "She said she wanted to make amends for all her unkindness to me. Then she told me I'd be foolish to pass up such a chance, that I'd never make it as an opera singer if I was afraid to take risks. She said if I didn't take the roles it would be all over Venice that I'd refused to step in when help was needed. She assured me she was only telling me all this as a friend. She filled me with confidence that I could do it, and that you'd be pleased."

My words were peppered with choking sobs. I twisted my handkerchief and stared at the floor. I couldn't look at him.

He groaned, and I could hear the anger in his voice. "*That little minx*. Is there no end to her intrigues? How could you be so gullible, Annina? By now you should have learned she's no friend of yours. She's no friend to anyone, not even to herself. She's her own worst enemy."

Fear gripped my heart. He'd lost confidence in me, like he had in Chiara. I didn't think I could bear it. I covered my face with my hands and wept helplessly.

I felt him pull my shaking body into his arms.

"Don't cry," he said, his voice a little gentler. "You'll only strain your voice more."

This brought a new gush of tears. I leaned into his shoulder and tightened my lips to stop their quivering. After a moment I pulled back. Lifting my eyes to his, I asked the question I had to ask.

"Do you still want to be my teacher?"

He didn't answer right away. He gazed at me, frowning, and the chill of dread swept through me like a blizzard.

Then, ever so slightly, his eyes softened. "Yes, I do," he finally said.

The warm balm of relief calmed the blizzard. I sighed deeply and felt my whole body relax.

Don Antonio cocked his head slightly, and a faint smile passed over his lips. "I don't mean to be harsh, Annina. I only want the best for you. I've seen too many over-anxious young singers burn themselves out before they had a chance to get started. I don't want that to happen to you."

"Will you help me?" I asked, dabbing my eyes with my drenched handkerchief.

"Yes, I'll help you. But you must be willing to commit to a regimen of intense technical study. We already know you have a dramatic gift. That'll still be there when you've perfected your craft. If you'll do my bidding, adhere to my instruction, and allow me to help you develop your vocal skill to match your natural talent, you'll have the critics at your feet."

"Do you really think so?" My heart soared with renewed hope. "Oh, I'll do anything you say, maestro, I promise."

He looked at me thoughtfully. With a kindly smile, he said, "I can see I'm going to have to keep a close eye on you from now on."

My eyes and cheeks were still wet with tears, but I couldn't keep the corners of my mouth from curling up. Moments ago I was afraid he'd never want to see me again, and now he didn't want me out of his sight.

"When shall we start our lessons again?" I asked, wiping my nose with the back of my hand.

"I have some business to take care of today. We'll start tomorrow. Plan to come at your usual time."

Then he looked at me half reprovingly, half curiously. "I won't ask how you got here today. But I'll walk you home." He put his arm around me, and I welcomed its familiar comfort.

DON ANTONIO WAS PATIENT with me over the next few weeks. At my lessons he took me gently through easy technical exercises to repair my strained voice and restore its clarity and suppleness. Slowly, not only my voice but my lost self-confidence came back. Best of all, Chiara resumed her unexplained absences from Signora Malvolia's house, and without her meddling my lessons went smoothly. Finally, I was free of Chiara's entrapment.

Then one evening Signora appeared at my bedroom door, looking flustered. "*Annina*, you have an important visitor." She bustled back downstairs before I had a chance to ask who it was.

I smoothed my hair and dress and hurried to the parlor. My heart lurched when I saw the duke.

A grin lit up his face. "Signorina Annina, what a delight." Oozing charm and elegance, he bent and kissed my hand.

"Your Excellency." I lowered my eyes and curtsied.

"I only just arrived in town and decided to take this opportunity to pay a call on my enchanting protégée." Gripping my hand, he ran his eyes over me.

I felt myself flush.

"I didn't think it possible, Annina, but you grow lovelier every time I see you."

"Thank you, Excellency." I withdrew my hand and dropped another curtsy.

"Now, now, you needn't be bashful. After all, you're not a little girl anymore. You're practically a woman."

Signora appeared with a carafe of brandy and glasses on a tray. "Your Excellency!" she gushed, in a nervous, unnaturally high-pitched voice. She set the tray down and flittered about. "May I pour you a glass?"

"Thank you, Signora Malvolia, I'd like to speak with Signorina Annina alone."

"Oh, of course. Certainly, Excellency." She scuffled out of the room and pulled the parlor doors closed.

I clasped my hands in front of me. "Your visit is an unexpected pleasure, Excellency."

"Yes, it is a pleasure indeed." He poured a glass and

held up an empty one to me, his eyebrows raised.

I shook my head.

He sauntered back over to me with his drink in hand and his mouth set in a confident smile. Taking my hand once more, he very lightly stroked my palm with one of his fingers. I stiffened and felt my flesh creep. He downed his brandy in a single gulp and went to refill his glass. I clasped my hands again, my knuckles rigid with tension.

"Let us sit, Annina, and I'll tell you why I've come."

He sank onto the only upholstered piece of furniture in the room, a settee covered in faded damask. He patted the cushioned seat and gave me an inviting look. Reluctantly, I slid in beside him.

"I heard you made quite an impression at the San Moisè recently," he said. "I'm sorry I had to miss that."

I stared at my clenched hands. "Well, I—"

"Don't be modest, my love." His hand was caressing my shoulder. I shrank from him, and he glanced at me in mock reproach. "There's no need for alarm, sweet girl. I think you'll be pleased at what I have to say."

An inkling of curiosity made me look his way.

"A budding prima donna such as you should have her own private domicile. Thus I've decided to remove you from this gloomy boardinghouse and set you up in a private apartment, under my protection of course."

"By your *protection* you mean . . ."

"That I'll pay your rent and all your expenses, naturally."

My heart fluttered with excitement. "Oh, Your Excellency, this is much too generous."

His smile was gallant. "Nothing is too generous for such a beautiful, talented young lady as you, Signorina Annina."

I dismissed all my foolish fears. He really did mean well, I felt sure of that now.

AT MY LESSON the following afternoon I could hardly wait to tell Don Antonio the news.

"The duke wants me to move out of Signora's house. He says he'll pay for me to have my own apartment."

He looked alarmed. "I don't think that's a good idea, Annina."

"Why not? You know how much I hate that wretched boardinghouse. The duke has offered to give me a place of my own to live and money to live on."

"You can't take money directly from him! Do you know what he'd then expect of you?"

I blinked with uncertainty. "What?"

He sighed. "You're very innocent, my dear. Let me make this clear. He'll expect to share your bed as well as your operatic triumphs."

My cheeks burned so hot I thought they were on fire.

"I'm sorry to be so blunt, but it's important you understand this," he said.

In spite of my embarrassment, I felt defiant. "I'm not a child. I'm old enough to have my own home."

"Annina, you must listen to me. Venice isn't a safe place for a young girl to be alone. Who would protect you?"

I felt angry and hurt that the conversation had gone in such a different direction than I'd expected. I crossed my arms and frowned, my lip quivering.

"Be reasonable, Annina. Do you want to end up like Chiara?"

So *that* was it. He was disturbed about Chiara's loose ways and afraid I'd end up following the same path.

I lifted my chin. "You know I'm nothing like her."

"The duke doesn't, though. If you accept payment from him on those terms he'll think he owns you."

Inwardly I squirmed with chagrin at his implication. But I was determined not to let him see my discomfort. I pulled my handkerchief from my sleeve and squeezed my fists around it.

"You're wrong, maestro, he's not like that at all. He really wants to help me build my opera career."

He almost laughed, and I noticed I'd twisted my handkerchief into a knot.

"Annina," he said, with an obvious effort to calm his voice. "For your own good I must tell you this is wrong.

The arrangement he's proposed would be ruinous for you. Your operatic success is not his first priority. He wants to use you for his own ends. And if you insist on staying under his dubious protection, I'm afraid I can't help you."

The sound of finality in his closing words frightened me more than anything he'd said before. I stared at him in flustered silence.

He must have taken my silence for defiance. He frowned, shook his head, and turned back to his score shuffling. "Do as you please, then. You don't need my permission to leave Signora Malvolia's house."

I felt defeated. "I know I don't need your permission . . . But . . ."

"You'd like my approval," he said, turning back to me.

"Yes."

"I'm afraid I can't give it."

My heart drooped. Then I had an encouraging thought. "I'll write my older sister. Maybe she could come live with me and be my chaperone. What about that, Antonio?"

I'd dared to drop his priestly title. He didn't seem to notice.

"Well . . . I suppose that's a possibility."

"I'll write to her today. I'm sure she'll be willing when she realizes how important this is to me."

"Hmm." He didn't look so sure. "Whatever your living arrangements, you must agree not to sing in any more public performances until I decide you're ready."

"Oh, I promise."

"And if the duke is to continue being your patron he must understand this and consent to it."

"He will, I'm sure. I'll make him understand. Or . . . maybe *you* could talk to him, maestro. He likes you, and he'll listen to you."

His smile was indulgent. "I think he likes my music more than he likes me. Nevertheless, I'll speak to him if you wish. I'll try to explain to him the folly of pushing you into a career before you're ready."

CHAPTER 17

Il Rio del Mondo Novo

The New World Canal

The duke left town again before Antonio had a chance to talk to him. But the day after he left, a messenger delivered a banknote to Antonio, signed by the duke, to cover my expenses for the next two months. And much to my joy, Paolina agreed to come to Venice for an extended stay.

On the day she was scheduled to arrive I waited anxiously at my bedroom window and watched the endless procession of gondolas that crowded the San Marco Canal. When a gondola carrying my sister finally glided into view, I scampered down the stairs and through the front door. The gondolier had just helped her from the boat, and I flew into her arms.

She pressed me to her, then pulled back to look at me. "Annina, Annina! Look at you. Where's the frightened little girl I bid farewell to so many months ago? Oh, my sweet baby sister." She was smiling, but her eyes shone with tears. "All I see is a lovely, confident young lady. I can't get over how you've changed, my little Annina," she said, drawing me to her again.

Antonio's sister Margarita had found us an apartment in the Santa Maria Formosa district, not far from the Vivaldis' house, and Paolina and I moved in the day she arrived. The furnished lodgings were on the second floor of a building that rose above the calm waters of the Rio Maria Formosa. The windows on the opposite side overlooked the *campo* Santa Maria Formosa, which opened out before the church of the same name.

Like every square in Venice, our *campo* was practically a village. The ground floors of the surrounding buildings housed shops and markets of all kinds: an apothecary, blacksmith, shoemaker, coffee shop, greengrocer, baker, butcher, and barber.

Our *appartamento* was small, just two rooms and a kitchen, but to me it seemed like a palace. Singing to myself, I hung my dresses in the wardrobe cupboard that stood near the bed my sister and I would share.

When Paolina left the bedroom for a minute, I quickly took *la moretta* from my trunk. "I'd better hold on to you, just in case," I whispered, as I tucked her in the back of the cupboard, behind my clothes.

That evening I was anxious to talk about my latest adventures. I didn't mean to, but I found myself telling my sister about Chiara's recent trickery and my troubles at the San Moisè.

She frowned her disapproval."*Santo cielo*, Annina, what mischief you get into if you don't have someone to look out for you every minute. I'm surprised Don Antonio isn't at his wits' end with you by now."

Knowing my sister, this scolding was to be expected and didn't bother me in the least. I grinned and shrugged.

BY EIGHT O'CLOCK the next morning our *campo* was bustling with activity. I opened the parlor window to the cool morning air and a colorful view crowded with balconies, shutters, and chimneys. Cages of chirping canaries, crowing blackbirds, and squawking parrots dangled over almost every balcony.

Housewives hung their laundry and gossiped from window to window. Below, rosy-cheeked water girls chattered and laughed while they drew buckets from the well. An old peasant woman, bent from carrying baskets of bottled milk, glowered at a rowdy pack of boys who surrounded her and rudely mimicked her hunched posture and crooked gait. She upbraided them in the name of all the saints and powers of darkness, and they scampered off, laughing uproariously. A carpenter made fragrant whittlings with this knife while he flirted with a shop girl, and a fisherman wandered the *campo*, hawking baskets of sole and mackerel with a tuneful cry of "Beautiful and all alive!"

I stepped out on the balcony and peered across the square toward the *Rio del Mondo Novo*, New World Canal, which led to Antonio's house. My heart spilled over with happiness. This "new world" was my dream coming true.

Paolina soon joined me, carrying a tray of steaming coffee with milk. We sat in comfortable companionship and sipped from our mugs, while streams of sunlight bathed us in the summer morning's gentle warmth.

Realizing I'd spent the whole evening before talking about myself, I was bursting with questions about home.

"Paolina, how's Papà?"

She sighed. "His health has improved, but he's in worse financial straits than ever. With you and Mamma gone he's been too depressed to run his business profitably."

My stomach agitated, and the sip of coffee I'd just swallowed turned bitter. I set my cup down.

"Why didn't you tell me this in your letters?"

"I didn't see any point in causing you distress, darling. There's nothing you could have done about it."

"But there *is* something I can do about it. I'll send Papà the little bit of money I earned at Treviso and the San Moisè. And I'm going to be making a lot more money soon, when Antonio starts giving me roles in his operas."

"*Antonio*?" My sister raised her eyebrows.

"Yes, that's what I call him now."

"I see. I didn't realize you and he had become so familiar."

"Oh, we have. I mean, I'm very comfortable with him. He treats me like family."

"Well, I suppose that's a good thing. But what were you saying about opera roles?"

My agitation changed to exhilaration. "Antonio said that in about a month I can start singing in private salon concerts and by autumn I might be ready to sing onstage in his operas. I'll be earning my own money on a regular basis, and nothing would give me more pleasure than to use that money to help you and Papà."

"That's awfully generous of you, Annina. But you're only a child. You shouldn't be burdened with supporting our family."

"It's not a burden. I *want* to help. Don't you see? In Mantua there was nothing I could do to help Papà. But here in Venice I have the chance to prosper with my music."

Paolina smiled at me, then looked down thoughtfully. "There's something else I should tell you."

"What?"

"Papà's heard from Mamma."

"*What?* When? Why haven't you told me this before? What did she say?" My insides were a whirlwind of joy and suspense.

"She's hoping for a reconciliation with Papà."

My heart leaped. "Paolina! This is the most wonderful news you could have given me."

She smiled kindly and reached over to squeeze my hand. "I'm glad, darling. But you mustn't get your hopes up too much. You know how temperamental Mamma can be."

"Yes, yes, I know," I said, as my soaring heart started to flounder.

CHAPTER 18

La Violenza

Violence

It was cold for July. A damp chill hung in the air and dark clouds loomed overhead. Paolina had gone to the market, and I sat gazing out the parlor window. Dusk blanketed Venice's spires and domes with a creeping gray mist.

Darkness quickly took over the lingering afternoon light, and a tremor ran up my back as if an icy wind had blown through the house. I lit the oil lamp in the hall and carried it to the bedroom.

Soon a hard rain started to fall. I wrapped in a thin shawl and sat on the wooden window seat that overlooked the Rio Maria Formosa. Poor Paolina. I hated to think of her caught in this downpour.

Shivering, I watched the gush of rain and listened to the rhythmic sound of icy drops pattering against the window. My gaze fell on the choppy waters of the canal, stirred to a frenzy by the gushing torrent.

A sharp knocking at the front door startled me. I picked up the lamp and hurried back to the hall. It must be Paolina, I thought. She's forgotten her key again.

But it wasn't Paolina. It was the duke.

"Your Excellency! I had no idea you were back in town."

"Yes, I'm sure you're quite surprised to see me," he said, without smiling. Before I could think what to say, he stepped inside and closed the door. "I'll get right to the point." He took off his dripping cloak and shook it out on the rug.

I shivered, but not from the dank cold he'd brought in with him. Again, I smelled liquor on him, and his usual roguish manner was darkened by an angry tinge. I felt a pricking sensation deep inside.

"I understand you've turned down all the operatic engagements I've arranged for you. May I ask what you have to say for yourself?"

The pale light of the oil lamp flickered, as did my insides. I placed the lamp on the hall table.

"Anto—my teacher has advised me not to accept any more opera engagements for now. He wants more time to work on my technical skill."

"Yes, I'm sure he does," he said, sneering. "Don't you know it's all over Venice what's going on between *il Prete Rosso* and his Annina? Have you any idea how much of a chump you've made me look?"

"*What?* What do you mean? I don't understand."

The color rose in his face. "I think you understand perfectly. Don't even bother with your innocent little girl act. I'm no longer fooled by your clever dramatics. By the way, how much of my money are you paying him?"

"I'm not paying him anything. He doesn't want money from me."

"Then what *does* he want? Do you expect me to believe the great Antonio Vivaldi would give up so much of his valuable time for a little nobody like you—for *nothing*? Come now, signorina. You insult my intelligence."

I wished Paolina would come home. I had a feeling something bad was about to happen.

The duke ground his teeth, and his eyes blazed. "Well aren't you going to say anything?"

"I think you should go," I said, trying to stay calm, but the tightness in my throat made my voice crack.

"Let me remind you, young miss, that your presence here in Venice is financed by *my* generosity. You have no right to dismiss me from the house I'm paying for, or from your presence." He grabbed my arm and roughly pulled me to him.

I writhed and fought to free myself from his strong

grip. "Let me go! My sister will be home any minute!"

There was no stopping him. He crushed my body to his and fastened his hot mouth on mine. I felt him throbbing and trembling, and panic overtook me. Pressing my fists to his chest, I managed to push away from him. Before I could catch my breath, he smacked me hard across the mouth with the back of his hand. I staggered backward and shrieked in pain as tears flooded my eyes. My hand flew to my mouth, which was already wet with blood.

Instantly his fury seemed to vanish, and panting, he reached for me. "Annina, I'm—"

I didn't wait for the rest of his sentence. I ran to the front door, hurled it open, and darted down the stairs, into the frigid downpour. The usually busy *campo* was practically empty, except for a few cloaked figures who were running for cover.

Blinded by cold daggers of rain in my face, I bumped into a man who grasped my arm and said, "Can I help you, signorina?" Terrified, I pulled away from him and continued my flight across the now deserted *campo.*

I stopped at the Rio del Mondo Novo, gasping for breath. Rain poured harder than ever and it was starting to thunder. The waters of the canal churned with a terrible violence, and there wasn't a gondola in sight. I was alone, completely drenched, and so chilled I could hardly move. I stood for a moment hugging myself, my teeth chattering. Blinking the rain out of my eyes, I realized I was a very short distance from the Ponte del Paradiso.

I sloshed through icy puddles and made my way to the bridge. The wind off the canal nearly blew me over, but I gripped the bridge's concrete railing, climbed its slippery steps, and inched my way across. Soon I was on solid ground again, and just a few steps from the Vivaldis' house. I made my way to the front door and pounded with all my strength.

Margarita opened the door, and her jaw dropped at the sight of me. She pulled me out of the rain. "Annina! *Dio mio*, what has happened to you?"

I was shaking too hard to speak.

"*Antonio!*" she called, her voice shrill with fright. "It's Annina! She's been hurt!"

He appeared from his study in shirtsleeves, his sandy hair falling around his face. His eyes widened with alarm when he saw me.

I ran to him and pressed my face to his shoulder. "You were right, I should've listened to you," I said in a muffled voice.

"About what?"

"About the duke."

He held me close for a moment, then gently clasped my upper arms and stepped back to examine my face. The blood oozing from my lip had soaked through his white shirt, and so had the wetness from my dress and hair, but he didn't seem to notice. With a troubled look, he took out his handkerchief and dabbed carefully around my lips.

The corners of his pinched mouth twitched. "Did he do this to you?"

My trembling lip made it impossible for me to speak, so I just nodded.

Antonio's jaw tightened.

Margarita stood nearby making the sign of the cross and wringing her hands. "*Antonio,*" she said, "I must get the poor child out of these wet clothes before she catches her death."

"Yes, find her something dry to put on," he said.

Margarita drew me away from him, and I let myself be guided by her firm hands into a little bedchamber off the kitchen. With much fretting and tongue clucking she had me dry, cleaned up, and wrapped in a soft robe within minutes. She combed out my damp hair and left it hanging loose around my shoulders.

"Now go talk to Antonio while I fix you a nice pot of tea," she said, patting my arm.

Teary-eyed and shaky, I went to the parlor and found him pacing and fastening up a fresh shirt.

"I'm sorry about your shirt," I said.

"Never mind about that. Come, Annina, have a seat and tell me what this is all about."

I curled up on the sofa, tucking my shoeless feet under

me and wrapping my arms around myself to ease the bone-rattling chill that shook my body. He picked up a *copriletto*, a coverlet, from a nearby ottoman and tucked it around my shoulders.

"Thank you, Antonio," I said, shaking as much from pain as from the cold. Margarita had managed to stop the bleeding from my lip, but it still smarted.

"Try to tell me what happened," he said, sitting on the ottoman, his hands clasped between his knees.

I looked at him with eyes that felt like they were melting in salty liquid. "Paolina went to the market, and I was home alone. Then the duke showed up and asked me a lot of questions. I was scared and told him to leave, but he wouldn't."

Antonio's brow darkened. "What did he do to you?"

I started to cry, and he rushed to my side. He took my hand, and I leaned my wet face against his shoulder. My throbbing lip brushed the crisp, fresh smelling fabric of his shirtsleeve as I went on. "He grabbed me and tried to kiss me, and when I pulled away from him, he hit me. Then I ran out the door and came here."

My body trembled even more at the memory of the duke's sweaty hands on me and the smell of liquor on his breath. I clutched Antonio's sleeve and squeezed my eyes against the tears that welled once again.

"Is that all?" he asked.

I nodded and pressed my cheek to his shoulder.

"It's all right now," he said, patting my hand. But there was an agitated edge to his voice, and I could feel his body tense with anger.

Margarita came in with a tea tray. "Here we are, my little lamb, this will help warm you up."

There was an anxious knocking at the front door. Margarita put down the tray and hurried into the hall.

"That must be Paolina. I sent a gondola to fetch her," Antonio said as he rose to greet her.

My sister looked like she was going to burst into tears when she saw me. I reached for her, and she hurried over and took me in her arms. "My poor, poor darling!"

I let myself melt into her protective embrace.

"That monster! What are you going to do about this?" she said, glaring up at Antonio.

He looked at us as if he were deciding what to say. Then he sighed. "I could have him charged with assault and arrested tonight."

"Would he go to prison?" I said, between sniffles.

"Most likely. And there'd be a trial."

"Would I have to go?"

"Yes. And since this is a criminal case, I'd hire a lawyer for you. But you'd have to tell the magistrate yourself exactly what happened."

"Would other people be there?"

"I'm afraid so. Criminal trials are open to the public, and something like this could turn into quite a spectacle."

I gazed at him in dismay. There was a brief silence, except for Margarita, who sat nearby whispering over her rosary beads.

Paolina squeezed my hand. "Do you really think that's advisable?" she asked Antonio.

He sighed again and rubbed his forehead. "No, I don't. As much as I hate to see that brute get away with this, I wouldn't want to arm the scandalmongers. They could cause far more harm than he has."

"Then how can we protect Annina from him?"

"Don't worry, I'll take care of it," he said.

"*How?*" I asked.

"I'll write to the duke and inform him that you'll no longer accept his patronage. That should end the problem, God willing."

Tears of panic filled my eyes. "But Antonio, how will Paolina and I pay our rent? How can we live? How can I help my father, like I've promised?"

"Relax, Annina," he said. "You'll be earning your own income soon enough. In the meantime, I'll cover your expenses."

I sighed shakily.

LATER THAT NIGHT, my mouth bruised and swollen, I pulled *la moretta* from her secret place in the wardrobe cupboard. Paolina was in the parlor, busy with her stitchery.

My fingers caressed the plush darkness of *la moretta*'s velvet face, and I murmured to her. "If I were wearing you, would you have protected me from the duke?"

But her silent stare gave me no answer. Closing my fingers around the muzzling *bottone*, revulsion came over me. I flung *la moretta* back into the wardrobe, closed it firmly, and pressed my forehead against the cupboard's wooden door. "You do nothing to protect me, but you plot to silence me. You've crippled my lip—my voice's threshold to the world. I should throw you into the canal and forget I ever laid eyes on you!"

But the memory of *la chiromante*'s words kept me from carrying out that threat:

The silence of la moretta will shield you.

CHAPTER 19

Il Gondoliere

The Gondolier

I made Paolina promise not to tell Papà, Graziana, or *anyone* about what had happened. Even though it wasn't my fault, I'd feel mortified if others heard about the shameful incident.

If anything at all valuable came out of my unfortunate run-in with the duke, it was the realization that I was attractive to the opposite sex. The idea started to form in my mind that this could be helpful. And I certainly needed help.

Ever since the "incident," it seemed like *I* was in prison. The warm comfort I'd felt at Antonio's house the night the duke assaulted me had become stifling. I wasn't allowed to go anywhere, and I could never be alone. I knew I had to find a way to free myself from this suffocating existence, or I'd go mad.

A few days later I found a way.

PAOLINA USUALLY WALKED with me across the Campo Santa Maria Formosa for my lessons, but on this particular afternoon she had a headache and decided to let me go on my own.

"I suppose you'll be all right," she said. "But I don't want you walking alone. You can go by gondola."

"Of course I'll be all right. I'm not a baby, you know."

Paolina pressed her hand to her aching head and went down the back stairs to hail a gondola. I stood at the door with my pile of scores while she gave the gondolier Antonio's address and payment for the gondola ride.

The boatman lifted his cap and grinned. He looked awfully familiar. After he'd handed me and my stack of music into the gondola, and we were off, I realized who he was.

"I know you," I said.

He seemed pleased. "Is that so, miss?"

"Yes, you gave my sister and me a ride from the boat, when we first arrived in Venice last January."

"Hmmm." He eyed me curiously. "I'm not sure—"

"Don't you remember? I wanted my sister to take me

to the opera, and you helped me talk her into it."

His face brightened. "You can't be that girl who told me she'd come here to study music and sing in the opera."

"Yes, that's me."

"Well what do you know, miss, I almost didn't recognize you."

"And everything you predicted that night has come true. Well, almost. I've been studying with Don Antonio. That's where you're taking me right now—to his house for a singing lesson. I've already sung in several public performances, and I'll probably make my debut soon in one of his operas here in Venice."

"Is that a fact? Well I'll be, miss."

The man seemed so nice, and so trusty. I gave him what I hoped was my most winning smile.

"Do you mind if I ask your name?" I asked.

"Not at all, miss. I'm Fortunato."

"What a nice name. *Piacere*, Fortunato, I'm very pleased to make your acquaintance. I'm Annina."

He almost seemed to blush. "Likewise, Miss Annina."

"Fortunato, I can see you're a true gentleman, the kind of man a girl can trust."

He drew himself up proudly. "I'd like to think so, Miss Annina."

"So I hope you won't mind if I ask your advice about something."

"If it's advice you need, miss, you've come to the right fellow."

"I knew it. Do you think it's safe for a girl like me to go around Venice unescorted?"

"A pretty young thing like you? Oh no, miss, that would be most unwise. You have no idea of the shady characters out there just waiting to . . . uh . . . take advantage of a sweet girl like you, Miss Annina."

I said nothing, but merely cast my eyes down.

"If you don't mind my asking, Miss Annina, how did you get that swollen lip?" He sounded genuinely concerned.

I'd almost forgotten about my hurt lip. I raised my fingertips to it. "Oh, that's nothing. Just a silly accident."

"You should be more careful, miss. It wouldn't do at all to mar that pretty face of yours." He peered at me with a vaguely worried look. "If you'll allow it, miss, I have a suggestion for you."

"Oh?"

"You need someone to look out for you. Your teacher is a very busy man, obviously. And as far as I can see, you have no other man in Venice to escort you around. I can also see you're the kind of girl who doesn't take to being cooped up at home."

"You're so right. What a clever man you are, Fortunato."

He straightened, and squared his shoulders. "Well, I

don't like to brag, miss. But I must say I've been known to have a few bright ideas from time to time."

"Of course you have, you're so astute. So tell me, what's your suggestion?"

"Well, miss, I'd like to offer you my humble services. I can take you to and from your lessons and escort you wherever you'd like to go. And mark my words, miss, you'll be perfectly safe with me. If any lewd looking fellow bothers you, I'll pound him into the pavement!"

I looked at Fortunato's muscular, sun-darkened arms and had no doubt he was capable of keeping his word. I wondered how old he was, but decided it would be impolite to ask. Studying his face I realized his weathered skin probably made him look older than he actually was.

"Why Fortunato, you're too kind. And so brave. But are you sure it wouldn't be too much of a bother for you?"

He gave me his brightest smile. "Certainly not, Miss Annina. It'd be a pleasure."

"I'll pay you, of course."

"Well, miss, I hadn't even thought about that. But a few *soldi* now and then might help keep me honest," he said, chuckling.

I smiled at him and giggled. Then I realized we were pulling up to Antonio's house.

Fortunato leaped off his perch and with great gallantry handed me and my stack of music out of the gondola. I turned toward the door, but he rushed ahead of me with my scores in his arms, and said, "I'll announce you."

When Margarita opened the door, Fortunato took off his red cap and lifted his chin with an air of importance. "Announcing Miss Annina . . . uh . . ." He looked back at me, his forehead puckered.

"Girò," I whispered, leaning toward him.

"Miss Annina Girò is here for her lesson with Don Antonio Vivaldi."

Margarita ushered us into the hall. "I'll let him know Annina has arrived." She gave me a curious glance.

I thought Fortunato would have left by now, but he continued to stand in the hall, grinning, and holding my pile of music. Margarita hurried toward the study, and a moment later Antonio appeared, adjusting his collar.

"Annina, what—Oh, hello," he said when he spotted Fortunato.

"What an honor this is, maestro! I've long been an admirer of your operas. Please allow me to introduce myself. I am Fortunato, sir, at your service as well as that of your charming student, Miss Annina."

"Well, thank you, um—"

"I know you two have important work to do, so I'll take my leave." He turned to me and grinned. "Miss Annina, when shall I return for you?"

"In two hours, please."

"I'll be here." He handed Antonio my stack of scores,

bowed ceremoniously, and departed.

"What on earth was all that about?" Antonio asked. "Who is that man?"

"That was Fortunato, my gondolier," I said, trying to sound nonchalant.

"*Your* gondolier?" He gave me a reproachful look. "Annina, what are you up to now? And why are you out alone? Where's Paolina?"

I was feeling too good about things to be put off by his stern questions. "Paolina's home with a headache, and—"

"Oh, I see. I'm sorry she's not well."

"So she hailed a gondola and decided it was all right for me to come here by myself. And as soon as we were off I realized I knew the gondolier. He's the one who brought Paolina and me into Venice my very first night here."

The corners of Antonio's mouth tightened. "This isn't convincing me that—"

"Wait, let me finish. We started talking, and he remembered me too. He realizes I don't like to be cooped up, so he offered to escort me wherever I want to go."

Antonio closed his eyes and sighed. "After what happened last week I'd think you'd have learned to be more cautious. We don't know anything about this Fortunato character, and—"

"But I *do* know him. We talked a *lot*. He's really nice,

and a gentleman, and he wants to protect me."

I was getting more wound up, and Antonio was losing patience.

"Annina, this conversation is absurd and has gone far enough. When the gondolier returns, I'll tell him you won't need his services after all."

"No, Antonio, please don't tell him that. Won't you at least talk to him? *Please*? Once you do, I'm sure you'll agree he's completely trustworthy. I just can't live like this anymore. It's making me crazy. I might as well be in prison."

He looked at me, frowning. Finally he said, "All right, Annina. If it means that much to you, I'll talk to him. But I'm not promising anything."

Antonio's talk with the gondolier later that afternoon went well, and Fortunato soon became a trusted protector and friend. Things were looking up again.

THE FOLLOWING SUNDAY, Antonio invited Paolina and me to a concert his students were giving at the Pietà. These concerts were held every Sunday and holiday. Venetians from all walks of life, along with visitors from far and wide, came in throngs to hear Antonio's famed *figlie di coro* whenever they performed.

As we entered the crowded hall I looked up to see

about two dozen girls and young women, all in red gowns. They were only partly visible behind the lattice-work that shielded their performance loft, but I could see that each of them held an instrument. I strained my eyes and noticed violins, cellos, mandolins, flutes, oboes, bassoons, and several other instruments I couldn't name.

Soon Antonio appeared in the priestly cassock he always wore at the Pietà. Movements behind the latticed screen looked shadowy, but I could see everyone position their instruments to begin. The music that started a moment later was anything but shadowy. Brightly colored and wildly exciting tones filled the room and moved at such a lively pace my ears could hardly keep up. More instrument sounds than I'd ever heard flooded my eager senses. It sounded so exciting and fun.

Yet these young women's technical precision and professionalism were astounding. I almost envied them, but the joy their music stirred in my heart prevented me. Antonio was indeed a gifted teacher, and I was grateful his gifts could be shared with so many.

THE NEXT DAY Paolina and I received word from Papà that Mamma was at last coming home. To help smooth things over between them, Paolina decided to return to Mantua for a short visit. I ached to go with her but contented myself with writing a letter to my mother:

Dearest Mamma,

My heart has been bursting with happiness since I heard you're coming home.

When you left, my heart was filled with overwhelming sorrow. In truth, much of my sorrow was caused by the fear that my unruliness was the reason for your departure. I pray you'll forgive me and restore the loving bond that ties my heart to yours and yours to mine.

I'm pleased to tell you I have the honor of studying with Don Antonio Vivaldi, and I'm hopeful that I'll soon prosper with my music. In the event that God grants me this success, I'll never neglect to share my good fortune with you and Papà.

Mamma, I hope you know this letter is written in good faith, and that the sentiments I express show in some small way the countless feelings of love and respect I have for you. I pray that you find in Papà, Paolina, and me the life you long to have, always in companionship with your loving family.

Your daughter, who loves you more than herself,

Annina

As much as I longed to see Mamma, I couldn't leave Venice because Antonio and I were engaged for a series of private performances. The first of these events was a concert at the Venetian home of Antonio's Bohemian patron, Count von Morzin.

Graziana, who'd come to stay with me while Paolina

was away, spent that day fussing over me. Early in the afternoon she washed my hair, rinsed it with lavender water, and brushed it dry by the kitchen hearth. One advantage to my fine, silky hair was that it didn't take long to dry.

I sat by the fire wrapped in a warm dressing gown, and worrisome thoughts nettled my brain. "Graziana, my throat feels prickly. What if my singing's terrible?"

"Don't be silly. Of course you'll sing beautifully. Don Antonio wouldn't let you do this if he wasn't sure you're ready."

"I don't know why I'm so nervous."

"You should feel excited."

"I *am* excited, but I'm also afraid."

"Now stop this, Annina. I'm going to make sure you look so beautiful, the audience will be mesmerized by you. Your singing will only dazzle them all the more."

"I wish I could feel as confident as you do."

When my hair was dry, Graziana brushed it till it shined and coaxed my wayward locks into ringlets with the curling irons she'd been heating over the fire.

I put on my underclothes, and Graziana brought out the new dress she'd designed and made for me—a silk gown of eggshell white, with a lace bodice and rose-colored sash. The bodice angled down from the waist, in the latest fashion, and the skirt fell in graceful folds down to the floor. The dress's slightly off-the-shoulder sleeves were snug around my upper arms and flared out gracefully just above the elbow, falling about halfway down my forearms.

After she'd helped me into my dress, Graziana went back to work on my hair. She pulled most of the curls back and up, and tied them with rose-colored silk ribbons. I'd never felt so elegant and grown-up.

I was sorry I didn't own any jewelry, but Graziana assured me I looked fine without it. "Never mind, Annina, jewelry is for faded old matrons. Pretty, fresh-faced maidens like you don't need it."

Fortunato was bringing Antonio to fetch me, so we could go to Count von Morzin's *palazzo* together. When I came into the front hall, Antonio had just arrived. He was dressed simply but tastefully, in a black broadcloth frock coat and priest's collar. His reddish-gold hair fell past his chin in loose waves.

"Annina, you look lovely. The count's guests will be completely enchanted by you," he said.

"I hope you're right." My stomach flittered as he placed my cloak around my shoulders

Graziana stood at the door to see us off, and I noticed her and Fortunato exchange bashful smiles.

But I was too anxious about the concert to give that much thought. I was thinking about the audience's reaction to the first aria I'd sung at the San Moisè a few months before. The grimaces. The mocking sneers.

I tried to give Antonio a confident smile. But fear crept through me, and I felt every muscle in my body go rigid.

CHAPTER 20

L'Esilio

The Exile

I walked into the grand salon of Count von Morzin's *palazzo* on Antonio's arm and gaped at the sumptuousness that surrounded me. My eager eyes drank in the throngs of elegantly dressed people who seemed to float about the room, chattering, laughing, and clinking glasses.

The men's embroidered waistcoats, trim knee breeches, and powdered wigs paled in comparison to the lavishness of the women's finery, which glittered in more colors and designs than I'd ever imagined. The room's towering walls and soaring ceiling were clothed in even more splendor. Almost every inch was covered in ornament or fresco.

Many curious eyes turned our way. I noticed hand-guarded whispers, especially among the women, along with flashing glances directed at me. Then I spotted the duke across the room. He held a glass of brandy and eyed me coolly. I looked away and clutched Antonio's arm more tightly.

Out of the corner of my eye I saw a glamorous, bejeweled blond woman step close to the duke. I turned my head slightly in their direction and couldn't believe my eyes. It was Chiara. She flashed me a scornful smile and slipped her hand through the duke's bent arm.

The room became stifling. My heartbeat quickened, and sweat dripped down the inside of my bodice and between my breasts. I pressed closer to Antonio and looked up at him anxiously. His attention was completely taken up by his many admirers, who swarmed around him like bees to honey, prattling compliments and witticisms. Lately I'd tended to forget how famous he was. His fans must have wondered who this frightened looking ingénue was clinging to him. I prayed they'd forgotten about my bungled performances at the San Moisé.

Antonio slowly worked his way through the crowd, pulling me along. When we reached the performance area he patted my clinging hand, gently unfastened me from his arm, and ushered me to a nearby seat. He'd told me earlier that before my aria he was going to introduce one of his new concertos. I watched him joke with his musician friends, while my thoughts drifted back to Chiara and the duke. The image of their threatening glares loomed in my mind like a gathering storm.

My attention shifted back to the musicians as Antonio took up his violin and bowed a long, shimmering note. The room fell silent. The other players lifted their bows and matched the tone, and the harpsichordist played a sweeping flourish. Antonio gave his musicians a subtle but precise gesture to start the piece.

The concerto began with slow, peaceful music, tinged with an ominous calm. I felt myself being lulled into a dreamy, yet slightly edgy state. After a few phrases Antonio raised his violin to his shoulder and started a frenzied solo that jolted me out of my dreamlike mood and took my breath away. His fingers flitted across the strings with dizzying speed, and his facial expression was so intense he almost looked like he was in pain. Suddenly the rest of the string players joined him in a furious unison. Just as abruptly Antonio lowered his instrument, and the orchestra returned to its earlier peaceful theme.

Antonio lifted his violin to his shoulder again, and this time he played a solo that floated above the other instruments in a melody of such excruciating tenderness I thought my heart would melt. Before I could bask too long in that euphoric state, the music exploded once again in an even more turbulent frenzy. I felt I'd been swept up, helpless, into a violent storm. Only this storm was thrilling, not terrifying.

The corners of Antonio's mouth twitched and beads of perspiration dribbled down his temples. He was in such a furiously impassioned state I felt I hardly knew him.

I looked around and saw people sitting on the edges of their seats, spellbound. Wide-eyed women panted, their chests heaving as they fanned themselves. A girl of about sixteen swooned and nearly fainted. I turned my gaze back to Antonio and felt something close to adoration.

When the piece was over, he took out a handkerchief and mopped his face. The spectators were frozen in silence for an instant before they burst into applause. Antonio smiled his appreciation, gestured toward his musicians, and bowed. The applause went on.

Finally our host, the count, stepped forward, clapping vigorously. He laid an appreciative hand on Antonio's shoulder. "*Bravo*, maestro! Thank you for that sampling of yet another musical triumph from your prodigious pen and dynamical bow."

Antonio smiled and bowed courteously.

The count turned to his guests. "My friends, what you just heard is the first movement of Don Antonio's "Summer" concerto, from his brilliant new set of works, *The Four Seasons*. And now if I may, maestro, I would like to introduce your enchanting protégée. My friends, may I present La Signorina Annina Girò."

All eyes turned to me, accompanied by curious smiles and polite applause. My stomach twisted into a knot. I glanced at Antonio and saw that he too was smiling at me, and I felt a faint surge of confidence. He stepped over, and I slipped my trembling hand into his. He gave it an encouraging squeeze and led me to the front of the little ensemble. How in the world does he have the strength to go on? I wondered. And how can I possibly match the dazzling performance he just gave? Sharp pangs of anxiety jabbed my stomach when my eyes met Chiara's and the duke's smug stares.

The harpsichordist played the opening chord, and I burst into a stormy recitative:

Ah, the traitor will not listen to me!
Treacherous stars!
Have I not suffered enough to satisfy you?

I felt the words swell and burn inside me. Antonio lifted his violin to his shoulder and with a quick nod to the musicians started thrusting away at the aria's refrain. His music swept me into its embrace and held me fast. My voice intertwined and blended with the lilt of his violin as if we were a seamless sound, an indivisible expression.

My suffering spirit!

How can I break the arrow in my heart
since I adore the one responsible?

Tingling energy hung in the air, and for a moment the room was cloaked in deafening silence. The aria was over. My eyes darted to Antonio. His face shone with rapt serenity, as if he were caught in the magic of his own musical mind.

The room exploded with applause. People leaped to their feet with cries of *Brava! Bravissima!* Antonio took my hand, and I sank into a deep curtsy. The applause showed no sign of letting up. *Ancora una volta! Ancora una volta!* many shouted.

Antonio gripped my hand. "They want us to do it again!" He dropped my hand, snatched up his violin, and dived into the aria's introduction with renewed fury. I barely had time to catch my breath before I plunged once more into my opening verse.

ANTONIO WANTED TO LEAVE as soon as possible after the concert. We'd just stepped outside and were walking toward the gondola, when the duke appeared. My heart flinched, and I clung to Antonio's arm.

His hand fastened on my wrist. "Leave this to me," he said softly.

I stepped back obediently and crossed my arms across my chest, clutching the edges of my cloak.

The duke staggered slightly, and his voice was too loud. "Well maestro, I couldn't let you leave without congratulating you on yet another musical triumph!"

Antonio eyed him coldly. "You are too kind."

"Not at all, maestro. And please allow me to pay my compliments to your charming student."

An icy wind blew off the canal, and I pulled my cloak more snugly around myself.

The duke tried to approach me, but Antonio blocked his way. "Signorina Girò desires neither to see nor speak to you, sir."

"Surely you don't mean that, maestro." The duke's fuzzy tone had an angry edge.

Antonio turned to Fortunato, who hadn't taken his eyes off the two men. "Please help Signorina Annina into the boat."

"With pleasure, Don Antonio," Fortunato was quick to respond. He leaped off his perch and took me by the elbow. I let him hand me into the gondola, while I stared wide-eyed at Antonio and the duke.

The duke swaggered closer to Antonio. "So I see you're determined to keep her all to yourself."

Antonio visibly stiffened. "What is your meaning, sir?"

"I think you know what I mean, maestro," the duke said, with a cocky grin. "Do you expect me to believe you've never partaken of the charms of that enticing young lady, when she's obviously so attached to you?"

This was too much for Fortunato. With blazing eyes he made a move to get out of the boat, but I grabbed his arm and pulled him back. My instincts told me it was better to let Antonio handle this.

Antonio glared at the duke for a long moment, and I saw his fist clench. I held my breath.

Finally he said in a low, tense voice, "*May God forgive you for having such a thought.*"

The duke backed off without a word and sauntered toward the house. Antonio tightened his lips, shook his head, and turned to join me in the gondola. Fortunato rushed to assist him.

Once we were afloat, I felt safe and happy under the starry sky with my two protectors. Antonio was distant, though. He stared to the side, frowning, as if his thoughts were as deep and dark as the murky green waters of the Grand Canal.

I broke the silence. "What a pest he's turned out to be."

"He's more than that. He's absolutely incorrigible," he said, still gazing into the canal's gloomy depths.

"You're so right, Antonio. But you intimidated him. You always know how to put troublemakers in their place."

He turned to me with a half-smile.

I raised my eyebrows. "And did you see who he was with?"

"I did."

"What do you think about that?"

"I think they deserve each other."

The blunt wisdom of his remark sent me into peals of giggles. Antonio smiled at my giddiness, then laughed with me, softly.

In truth, I was tingling with the afterglow of the evening's success and bursting with eagerness to talk about it. The crisp night air on my face sharpened my excitement.

I grinned ecstatically at Antonio. "Your new concerto is amazing! It's the most thrilling, exciting music I've ever heard. Everyone there was completely enchanted. I'm sure they've never heard anything like it."

His smile brightened. "They haven't. No one has."

I hugged myself. "I knew it. Oh, Antonio, you're a genius! How do you think of music like that? I'm just astounded by how creative you are. I don't know how you do it."

My gushing praise seemed to please him, but he replied modestly. "I don't know how I do it either. My music simply comes to me. It's a gift from God."

"You're too modest, Antonio. That music comes from *you*. It *is* you."

He smiled again. "Which is another way of saying I'm abiding by God's will. But enough about me. Let's talk about your performance this evening. I can't tell you how moved I was by your singing tonight, Annina. You were stunning. When you sing my arias before a crowd you positively sparkle and shine. You breathe life into my music and make it your own. It's as if you become the music."

I grinned with happiness and hugged myself even tighter. It was the most wonderful thing he could have said to me. This was no empty flattery. He was likening me to his music, the thing that meant more to him than anything in the world. My heart overflowed with tenderness for him. "I'm so glad I pleased you, Antonio."

"I'm more than just pleased, Annina. I'm very proud of you. You sang with such fervor and sincerity, you charmed everyone in the room and completely won them over. It won't be long before you're ready to go onstage again—in one of my operas."

My whole body sizzled with joy.

GRAZIANA WAS WAITING up for me. "So how did it go?" she asked, her eyes bright with curiosity.

"It was wonderful!" I went on to tell her every tantalizing detail. When I got to the part about Fortunato's zeal to defend my honor when the duke became offensive, she grinned and blushed.

I paused. "What are you thinking, Graziana?"

"Oh . . . It's just that I find Fortunato so appealing, in a rugged sort of way." She giggled nervously.

"Graziana! Are you trying to tell me you've taken a fancy to Fortunato?"

"Well . . ." Her blush deepened. "I don't know. But I do get a strange tickly feeling inside when I look at his brawny arms."

This was fascinating.

"I noticed he gave you a certain look when you stepped outside earlier."

"Did you? Oh, Annina, do you think he likes me? I mean . . . well, he's not married or anything is he?"

"Not that I know of."

She was excited now. "You're so friendly with him, Annina. Do you think you could, well, you know, find out how he feels about me? Without letting him know I asked, of course."

I was delighted. I'd never been asked to play *Amore*, Cupid, before.

The next day, on the way to my lesson, I looked at Fortunato with a breezy smile. "What did you think of the dress Graziana made for my concert appearance last night, Fortunato?"

"It was splendid, Miss Annina. You looked lovely as an angel."

I beamed with pleasure. "Isn't she talented?"

"She is at that."

"Oh, Graziana's good at everything. I don't know what I'd do without her. No one could have a better or more loyal friend."

"Graziana's a dandy girl, I won't deny it," he said.

His candid grin told me all I needed to know.

ANTONIO GREETED ME with exciting news. "My negotiations for regaining managerial control of the San Angelo Theater are complete. I'll launch the new season in November, with my latest opera."

"Oh Antonio, how wonderful! Will I be singing in it?"

"You will indeed. The opera's called *Dorilla in Tempe*. It's about a princess, Dorilla, who against the will of her father and the gods is in love with a shepherd, Elmiro."

"Is Dorilla my role?"

"No. You're to play Eudamia, a nymph who's also in love with Elmiro and who spends most of the opera scheming to win him for herself."

"And does she get him?"

"She doesn't. But neither does Dorilla. Elmiro's accused of abducting Dorilla and is executed in the end by being chained to a tree and shot through with arrows. So Dorilla ends up marrying a herdsman, Nomio, who's really the god Apollo in disguise. Eudamia marries another shepherd, Filindo, who's been secretly in love with her and loyal to her throughout the story."

"How many arias will I have?"

"Three. One in each act. In the first, Eudamia expresses her yearning for Elmiro's love. In the second, she bemoans the hopelessness of her yearning. And finally, in the third, she pours out her rage to Elmiro for his rejection of her love."

My shoulders quivered with excitement.

He looked at me with a wry smile. "I have another piece of news I'm sure you'll be pleased to hear."

"What's that?"

"A retired singer from Venice, Signor Denzio, is putting together an opera company in Prague. He wants to hire Venetian singers and has asked for my help. I'm going to send him Chiara."

My jaw dropped. "How are you going to do that?"

"I've already asked for a meeting with her. Once she sees what a good opportunity this is she won't hesitate to sign the contract."

"I don't understand. Why should you do her such a favor?"

"To get her on the other side of the Alps, of course, where she can't cause us any more trouble."

I gazed at him in wonder. "That's so clever, Antonio. I never would have thought of it. But what if she won't go?"

"She'll go." His smile radiated confidence.

"How can you be so sure?"

"Because she's shrewd enough to realize Denzio's company is her best option. She has no prospects in Venice right now, or anyplace else for that matter. She's depraved herself to get back in favor with the duke, but she knows he'll soon tire of her. Trust me, Annina, Chiara won't turn down this opportunity."

In my mind's eye I pictured the magnificent mountain range on Venice's northern horizon. "Antonio, you said Prague is across the Alps? Where, exactly?"

"Far to the north, in Bohemia."

"How far?"

"Many hundreds of miles."

"It must be cold up there."

"Extremely. The climate should suit Chiara's temperament well, don't you think?"

We shared a smile.

A FEW DAYS later, I had a surprising visit.

CHAPTER 21

La Ninfa

The Nymph

I'd just finished my morning bath and was starting to dry my hair by the kitchen hearth. There was a knock at the front door, and Graziana went to answer. I heard muffled voices in the hall, then Graziana came back to the kitchen.

"It's Chiara," she said in an anxious whisper. "What would you like me to tell her?"

My heart quavered. "Invite her to sit, and tell her I'll be right there."

I looped the sash of my dressing gown, wrapped my damp hair in a towel, and went to the parlor to face Chiara. She had a look of desperation in her eyes, and her pinched mouth told me fury was lying just below the surface.

I tried to look composed. "Well, Chiara, what a surprise."

"I suppose you weren't expecting to see me again."

"No, I wasn't."

"I'll keep this short. I've come to warn you, Annina. To open your eyes to what you're getting into."

"I have no idea what you're talking about."

"You think you've finally triumphed. That you've defeated me and now, at last, everything will go your way." Her voice had a tense, almost strangled sounding edge.

I hesitated. "I hadn't thought about it like that."

Her eyes spit fire. "Then let me educate you! You think Don Antonio is some kind of saint. Well he's not. Just look what he's done to me."

"What he's done to you? He's done you a favor. Which is more than you deserve, if you ask me."

"A favor? Is that what you call it? I call it throwing his weight around to render me powerless. Shipping me off to his crony in Prague, as if I were a piece of livestock."

"What nonsense. Nobody's forcing you to go."

"You mean, you actually think I have a choice? Are you blind? Haven't you figured out yet how these impresarios, these smug tyrants, take control of our lives when we're young and vulnerable? How they use us for their own purposes then pass us around among themselves when it suits them? And your adored Don Antonio is no different. If I refuse to go to Prague he'll make sure I'm blacklisted at every theater in Italy."

"Did he tell you that?"

"Not in so many words. But I know he would. They're all like that." Her face took on the crimped expression of a peevish child. "I've been used, I'm telling you. Nobody cares about me." Angry tears filled her eyes, and she dabbed at them with a frilly lace handkerchief.

I felt more disgust than compassion for her sniveling self-pity. Hadn't *she* used others for her own ends, not to mention made my life a living hell for the better part of a year?

"I don't see how you can say that, Chiara. Don Antonio did everything for you—and you betrayed him."

She lowered her handkerchief to her lap and glared at me, her green eyes catlike. "What are you talking about?"

"You know exactly what I'm talking about. When he was forced out of his position at San Angelo you turned your back on him and sided with the people who were out to destroy him."

"And who, may I ask, told you that?"

My throat tightened. I wasn't about to betray Graziana's confidence. "No one had to tell me. I figured it out for myself."

Her eyes were fixed on me, and her mouth twisted into a tight, sinister smile. "Well, Miss Genius, let me tell you something. If you don't learn to look out for yourself in this business, *you* will be the one who's destroyed. Oh, I know you think you're safe and protected, because you're the Great Maestro's little darling right now. You think you're special to him, don't you? Well think again. You're just one in a long line. When you're no longer useful to him he'll pass you on to one of his cohorts. How do you think you'll feel then?"

I'd had enough. She could say whatever she wanted about me, but listening to her talk about him that way was more than I could stomach.

I stood abruptly. "I'm afraid I must end our visit. I have to finish drying my hair."

She breezed out with a cold, glittering laugh. I watched her silk skirts trail away as I closed the door firmly behind her.

Leaning against the closed door, I sighed with mingled revulsion and relief. The sting of Chiara's venom was softened by the near certainty that she was now out of my life forever.

PAOLINA RETURNED TO VENICE the following week. The minute she walked in the door of our apartment I started plying her with questions.

"Did Mamma come home?"

"Yes, she did," Paolina said, trying to catch her breath.

"Well? How is she?"

My sister looked at me with a weary smile and patted my arm. "What can I say, Annina. Mamma is still Mamma."

Dread crept through me. "Did you give her my letter?"

"Yes, I did," she said, sighing.

"And what did she say about it?"

"Nothing, I'm afraid, at least not to me."

"She must have given you a letter to bring back to me then," I said in a small voice, blinking hard to cool the sting of my tears.

Paolina smiled sadly and took me in her arms. "Please don't torture yourself like this, darling."

My spirits plummeted, and my soul wailed in torment as the realization came crashing down on me that my mother was incapable of love.

THE GHOSTLY MIST of approaching winter was a stark reminder that my first year in Venice was coming to an end. The misery I'd suffered those first wintry weeks here, which recently had been so far from my mind, now seemed chillingly close.

My anxious feelings were magnified at the first rehearsal of *Dorilla*, when I realized my role wasn't as significant as Antonio had made it sound. As *seconda donna*, the higher ranking singers looked down their noses at me. To make matters worse, they seemed jealous of my close relationship with Antonio and determined to put me in my place. The most trying of them was Maddalena Pieri, a contralto who specialized in male roles. Antonio had hired her to sing the part of Elmiro.

About two days into rehearsals I found myself alone backstage with Maddalena. She eyed me coolly, with barely concealed contempt.

"I had a letter from my friend Chiara Orlandi recently. She told me how you've bewitched Don Antonio into making you his exclusive protégée, to the point where you were able to persuade him to have her exiled to Prague."

My heart skipped a beat. "You know Chiara?"

"Yes indeed. And she's told me all about you and your secret relationship with *il Prete Rosso*."

"There's nothing secret about our relationship," I said, stiffening. "He's my teacher, and that's all there is to it."

Her smile showed her disbelief. "Well, if you expect anyone to believe that, you must be even more foolish than you are cunning."

I bristled with indignation, and my cheeks burned. "I don't have to listen to this," I said, and turned to walk away.

Maddalena's next words brought me to a halt. "I find it interesting that after all the fuss the maestro's apparently made over you, he's only given you the secondary female role in *Dorilla*."

Now my indignation was compounded by stinging humiliation. I was speechless, and to my horror, tears sprang to my eyes. Maddalena returned to the stage, obviously pleased with herself.

I couldn't talk to Antonio about this. After all he'd done for me I was afraid my complaints about Maddalena would sound like the whining of a spoiled brat. If I tried to get Paolina's sympathy, she'd only frown and shake her head in that *Didn't I try to tell you so?* way.

So I went to visit Graziana, who I hadn't seen much of since Paolina had returned to Venice. Ever since Chiara left for Prague I'd avoided Signora Malvolia's house. I was sure she blamed me for Chiara's "exile," and I had no desire to face her overblown accusations.

Fortunato delivered me to Signora's door, and she greeted me with a cold, quivering stare. I quickly made my way to Graziana's room. At the sight of me her face lit up and she rushed to embrace me. I poured out my story to her.

She smiled knowingly. "Most opera singers are self-centered, backbiting, and just plain mean-spirited. I learned that a long time ago when I started making costumes for them. Chiara, I must say, is an extreme case. But they're almost all like that to some degree. I think one of the reasons Don Antonio likes you so much is because you're *not* like that."

I felt the flicker of a warm glow inside, which almost immediately was clouded by doubt. "Then why has he given me a secondary role?"

"This is only a start, Annina. You're still very young. Those other singers are much more experienced, and you can only expect they're going to try to lord it over you."

"It's just so hard to take."

"Ignore them. Look at it this way—you're finally getting to sing onstage in Venice, in one of Don Antonio's operas. That's what you've been wanting, isn't it?"

"Yes, you're right," I said, sighing.

Graziana's eyes brightened with curiosity. "What kind of role are you playing?"

"I'm a nymph."

"A nymph? How appropriate. I'll design and make a costume that'll keep every eye on you, I guarantee it. Those high-flown singers will be so astounded when they see how gorgeous you look, their jaws will drop to the floor."

Now she was talking. I was starting to feel better already.

ON A CHILLY November morning, Graziana showed up at my front door. "I have a surprise for you," she said, pulling from her haversack what looked like a filmy piece of loose cloth.

"What's this?" I asked.

"Your costume, of course."

I held before me a sleeveless gown, whitish in color, made of a very thin, almost sheer fabric.

"That's just the main part of it," she said with a smile. "Here's the rest." She handed me a pale, flesh-colored silk chemise and matching stockings, a gauzy pink sash, and silk slippers the same shade as the stockings.

She grinned eagerly. "Why don't you try it on?"

I held the lovely but flimsy pieces of clothing in my hands and felt their delicate sensuousness. Weeks ago Graziana had measured me carefully for the costume, but she hadn't let me see it yet. She wanted to surprise me. I was more than surprised—I was stunned.

"Go on," she said. "I can't wait to see this on you!"

Reluctantly I went to my bedroom and slipped out of my clothes. Shivering, I put on the wispy little nymph costume. I had to admit that the clinging silk chemise, which barely reached halfway down my thighs, tickled my skin in a thrilling way, as did the silk stockings that hugged my legs so snuggly. The frail outer garment, cinched at the waist with the pink sash, draped softly around my body and fell in delicate folds down my legs to just above my ankles.

The sheerness of the fabric made everything subtly

visible that wasn't covered by the chemise. The little silk slippers completed the delicately alluring ensemble. I gazed at my image in the mirror. How, I wondered, can I wear this in public, on stage, in front of hundreds of people—in front of Antonio?

Hesitantly, I stepped out of my bedroom, hoping Graziana would agree the costume was too daring.

She glowed with pleasure when she saw me. "Annina, you look absolutely *gossamer*."

"Gossamer?"

"Yes! Light, delicate, ethereal. I asked around about nymphs when I was planning your costume and learned they're beautiful, fragile, semi-divine maidens who dwell in forests and country meadows. And that's you. As I look at you now, I'm convinced you *are* a nymph."

I wasn't sure if the goose bumps popping out on my skin were from the cold or the thrill that swept through me.

Graziana glanced down with a demure smile. "I had supper with Fortunato last night."

"Really? Where?"

"At the café near Signora Malvolia's house."

"And?"

She blushed. "I think he's sweet on me."

"That's wonderful!"

"I know he's a little rough on the outside. But he's really quite charming, don't you think?"

"Oh, I do. Fortunato's one of the kindest, bravest, most loyal men I've ever known. You and he are perfect for each other."

Her smile was euphoric.

THE DAY OF *Dorilla*'s premiere, Graziana spent most of the afternoon arranging my hair, applying my makeup, and making sure every tantalizing thread of my costume was perfectly in place.

My hairstyle was simple. Graziana tied the sides back with pink silk ribbons and let the loose strands fall around my shoulders, then placed a dainty wreath of tiny pink and white roses on my head. She decided my makeup should be light and understated so it wouldn't contrast too much with the graceful filminess of my costume. No one, not even Antonio, had seen the outfit yet, and I tingled with anticipation of the reaction I'd get.

Just before the opening sinfonia, Antonio came backstage to make sure everyone was ready. He looked at me almost in awe. "Annina, you're beautiful," he said, smiling boyishly, while the other female singers, especially Maddalena, glared at me.

I reminded myself that Maddalena's character, Elmiro, would be chained to a tree and shot dead with arrows near the end of the opera. The thought made me smile.

The opera went off without a hitch, and the audience clapped and hooted their praise when I made my bows. But I couldn't help feeling miffed about the little-girlishness of my role. I decided to speak to Antonio about it.

For all his sensitivity and attentiveness there were times, when he was absorbed in his work, that I felt invisible. The following afternoon was such a time. When I arrived at his studio he was writing furiously with ink-stained fingers, and his haste showed he was in a state of fevered inspiration.

I'd always respected Antonio's need for solitude when he was in the midst of creative frenzy. But today I felt too keyed up to be that considerate. I crossed my arms and fixed my eyes on him. The room was silent except for the frantic scratch of his pen across the music paper.

"Will you please listen to me?" I said.

He was oblivious to everything but the notes that seemed to want to fill the page faster than he could move his pen.

"Antonio!"

"Hmmm? What?" He glanced at me, absentmindedly.

"I'm trying to talk to you."

"What is it, dear?"

"Why do you keep putting me in these little child roles?"

"Because you *are* a child."

“I’m almost sixteen!”

“Are you? I thought you were still fourteen.”

I gave a loud sigh and raised my eyes heavenward.

He put down his pen and smiled. “All right, Annina. Why don’t you sit and tell me exactly what it is you’re trying to say.”

I was too restless to sit, so I strode about and gestured manically with my hands. “I want to play someone glamorous and sophisticated. Not only that, but someone who’s fighting injustice and not afraid to stand up for herself. I don’t want to be some meek little nymph or shepherd who sings sweet little songs about love and nature. I want to play characters with violent, mixed up feelings, and I want to sing music that’s full of passion and movement. I know you can compose music like that. I’ve heard it. So why won’t you create music like that for me? You’ve always said I fill my performances with sincere emotion and energize your music like no one else can. I want the chance to do that onstage!”

Out of breath, I paused, my heart in a flurry. He gazed at me with fascination in his eyes. I felt myself soften under his gaze, but I wasn’t ready to let go of my agitation.

I crossed my arms again. “Well?”

He cleared his throat. “Well—you’ve certainly made your point.” He stared down at his manuscript and seemed to be deep in thought. Finally he said, “I have some ideas I think you’ll be pleased with, Annina. But I’d like to wait and continue this discussion tomorrow, if you don't mind."

I was impatient to hear his ideas but realized I'd probably pushed things far enough for one day.

CHAPTER 22

La Malevolenza

Malevolence

The next day I couldn't get to my lesson fast enough.

When I arrived Antonio wasted no time getting to the point. "Annina, I feel you're almost ready for a truly challenging role."

I waited anxiously for him to go on.

"There's something you must understand, though. Like I've told you so often in the past, you have all the dramatic tools you need to portray emotionally complex characters convincingly. But your vocal technique still needs work."

My heart sank, and I felt my face droop.

His tone and expression became more animated, and he started to pace about. "Don't be downhearted,

Annina. Opera singing is an art, and all art is a struggle between expressive freedom and craft. I'm caught in that struggle all the time with my composing. Why do you think I called my latest set of concertos *Il cimento dell'armonia e dell' inventione*, the contest between harmony and invention?"

I thought a moment. "Because your creative urges clash with the rules of composition?"

"Precisely. And that's the way it should be. The more intense the conflict, the more exciting the artistic product. Expressive instincts are a goldmine, but without the discipline of technical precision they remain formless and therefore useless. Do you understand what I'm saying?"

I nodded. As hard as it was to admit, I knew he was right. "But what about the challenging role you were getting ready to tell me about?"

"There's an opera I wrote several years ago, *Orlando furioso,* based on the epic poem by Ariosto. Do you know the story?"

I shook my head.

"It's about a Christian knight, Orlando, whose mission is to disempower an enchantress from the underworld, Alcina. In my original version, Orlando was the central character. Now I want to revise the opera and put Alcina at the heart of the story. To do this I'll have to rewrite all her texts and music in order to make her a more complex character, who the audience will sympathize with. I'm envisioning you in that role, Annina."

My heart started beating so wildly I thought it would leap out of my chest.

He went on. "You can turn the painful experiences you've had to your advantage with this role."

"Really? How?"

"By channeling your feelings, agonizing as they may be, into your art. You must allow your emotions to become the energies they really are."

"I'm not sure I understand."

"Well, for example, how did you feel when Tomaso denied you the chance to express your emotions in your singing?"

"Angry and frustrated. Also terrified I'd always have to hide behind a mask—that my true self would never be understood or accepted."

"And what about when Chiara pretended to be your friend, then betrayed you?"

"I hated her. I wanted revenge."

"This is difficult, I know, but what was your emotional reaction when the duke behaved so dishonorably toward you?"

I hesitated, and my jaw tightened. "What I felt at that moment was a level of fury like I'd never known—fear and rage rolled into a single feeling."

He eyed me steadily. "I want you to summon those feelings when you play Alcina. Sing the role through the filter of your own experience. You must become Alcina, but don't think of yourself as a wicked sorceress. Think of yourself as a misunderstood young woman with ardent yearnings that are doomed to remain unfulfilled. Your reactions to those unfulfilled longings alternate between grief and rage and culminate in the kind of fury you've just described."

Excitement built in me till I thought I'd explode.

That moment marked the beginning of one of the happiest times of my life. I eagerly tackled all the technical exercises Antonio assigned me and practiced with a fresh sense of purpose. With his help, all my painful memories became tools to shape and hone my vocal technique into something that transcended mere craft and sparkled with artistic splendor. Together, we developed a method of vocal expression that had the dramatic power needed to portray Alcina's stormy passions and tragic downfall.

Graziana got to work on my costume right away. She decided this time my attire should be provocative, as well as queenly and mysterious. I had no doubt whatever she came up with would be perfect.

As for my music, Antonio outdid himself. In the first two acts I had four arias, for which he wrote the words and music. I didn't have any arias in the third act, though. Instead, he wrote for me a series of fiery recitatives and *ariosos*, short snippets of melody that were like bursts of emotional energy. All the tension and tangled feelings that had been building in the first two acts played themselves out in these raging outbursts.

Opening night was magical. Earlier that day January's gloomy dampness had been driven away by a cold but sunny brilliance. By evening the cloudless heavens cast a luminous aura over Venice's San Angelo district that almost matched the gentle radiance of the theater's interior.

Shortly before curtain time I peeked from backstage at the dazzling spectacle of Alcina's enchanted island. The painted backdrop portrayed a garden of such flawless beauty it could only be compared to paradise. The soft, muted light of oil lamps gave a dreamlike atmosphere, while glittering candelabras from above depicted a starry sky. I'd never seen anything so exquisite.

I was already dressed and ready for my big entrance. My costume was a wasp-wasted gown of alluring violet. The dress had a daring, off-the-shoulder neckline and filmy sleeves that flowed to my fingers. The skirt was made of many layers of the sheerest silk, some of which clung to my hips and legs enticingly, and some of which fluttered about me freely. The gown made me feel as light and sparkly as a cloud of fairy dust.

Graziana had brushed my hair to a high sheen and arranged it in an elegant twist on top of my head. A silvery crown studded with glittering faux amethysts topped off the costume. The overall effect was exactly as Graziana had planned: seductively regal.

In the third act an element of mystery would be added to my costume when I donned a hooded black cloak, lined with purple satin.

As I waited anxiously in the wings, I heard familiar footsteps. It was Antonio. The orchestra was gathering in front of the stage, and in a few short minutes he'd join them for the introductory sinfonia.

His eyes and smile glowed. "Annina, you're absolutely stunning."

I was so happy I was afraid I'd get teary-eyed and ruin my makeup if I tried to speak.

He touched my cheek in a very tender way. "You're going to astound them."

His smile and his touch filled me with confidence. I took a deep breath and nodded.

"See you in a few minutes." He kissed my forehead lightly and hurried off.

A silky-toned voice startled me from behind. "What a *touching* scene."

I turned, and my blood ran cold. "*Chiara.*"

Her smile glistened with charm, but her eyes were hard. "Yes, it's me. Can you imagine it? Here we are, together again. You thought you were rid of me for good, no doubt." She clucked her tongue and shook her head. "And your devoted Antonio not even here to hold your hand and protect you. How unfortunate."

My fingers stiffened and folded into fists. "What are you doing here?"

Her smile became smug. "Prague is dreary, so I decided to return to Venice once my contract with Denzio was up." She looked me over with cool, appraising eyes. "It looks like I got here just in time."

In the dim backstage light her eyebrows took on a diabolical slant, and deep lines seemed to be etched around her mouth.

Both gave her a frighteningly sinister look. My fists tightened. "What do you want, Chiara?"

Her lovely, cold face came close to mine, and her voice was a sharp whisper. "To see you fail, of course."

My skin crawled at the feel of her hissing breath.

The orchestra was tuning up. The other singers were still in their dressing rooms but would soon be coming out for their entrances.

I glared at Chiara with burning eyes. "*Get out.*"

"Oh, I wouldn't dream of it," she replied smoothly. "To see you humiliated—brought low in all your radiant finery, hooted and jeered by a hostile audience—will be so thrilling." Her eyes brightened. "Best of all will be the look on Antonio's face."

I had a sick, quivering feeling. I could only think of a single question. "*Why*, Chiara?"

"Because I have nothing but contempt for you. You and your clever schemes. You're no singer, and everyone knows it." Her eyes narrowed and chilled, and her lips spread into an icy smile. "And deep down, Antonio knows it too. Tonight will bear that out."

"That's absurd," I said, my voice pinched.

"Is it? You're nothing but a trickster who's managed to bewitch him with your crafty wiles. It's no coincidence he was prompted to create for you the role of that evil seductress Alcina. She characterizes you perfectly. You have no real talent. Through a combination of guile and little girl charm you managed to wheedle Antonio into taking you under his protection. And you'll be the ruin of him. So I intend to teach you a lesson. Tonight you'll be exposed for the fraud you really are."

Why didn't I bring *la moretta* with me? I thought frantically. She might have protected me from Chiara's crippling words. But she also would have muzzled my voice. No matter. Chiara had done that without *la moretta*'s help.

My eyes turned with dread to the empty stage. Its glimmering lights seemed to darken as the shadow of terror descended over me with all its malevolent power.

CHAPTER 23

La Libertà

Freedom

The sinfonia began and singers started to assemble backstage. Chiara strolled off with a smile of glee.

Dazed, I walked onstage behind the closed curtain. Chiara had won. She'd shattered my confidence. With cold precision, she had roused all my worst fears. And she knew fear would ensure my failure.

My opening aria was the most brilliant and technically challenging piece Antonio had ever written for me. Exactly the kind of aria I'd been pleading for. I wouldn't be able to sing it. My throat and jaw were welded shut.

Terror pricked my insides with the piercing sharpness of a thousand spearheads. All my strength had been sucked out of me. I felt weak and helpless.

Channel your feelings, agonizing as they may be, into your art. Allow your emotions to become the energies they really are.

Antonio's voice was in my head. He was telling me to use my fear to fuel my dramatic power. All at once I knew: Chiara's evil plan had backfired. The rage and terror she'd ignited in my heart would give Alcina life and make her real.

The curtain rose, and Antonio raised his violin to launch the brisk introduction to my first aria. I gathered my skirts and moved with an imperious stride toward the footlights. My quivers of fear turned to tingles of delight as flickering candlelight from above danced in the folds of my gown and gave it a shimmering quality. I caught Antonio's eye, and the fire in his gaze shot through me. I became Alcina.

With queenly confidence I asserted my power, while revealing my underlying fear of Orlando:

His warlike gaze,
that spreads terror,
brings fear to my heart!

The aria sprang from my throat, from the very core of my being, with more vehemence than I ever knew was in me. All my anxieties melded and flowed through the words and music in a way that felt wonderful and excruciating at the same time.

I soared through the opera's first two acts, swept up in a fever of inspiration. I schemed to weaken Orlando's power by seducing his fellow knights, Ruggiero and Astolfo. Secretly, though, I grieved at my inability to find true love:

If only I too
could enjoy with the one I love
the peace my heart cannot find.

In the third act my lament turned to fury at the injustice of the gods:

My bow wishes to break you,
my torch to extinguish you,
savage, tyrannical god of love!

At the end, defeated by Orlando, I donned my hooded cloak and raged:

I will go down and call out of the depths
the evil furies from the ghastly abyss,
and I will ask the depths for vengeance
for my betrayed love!

Swooping my cloak about me with a violent flourish, I descended to the underworld in a cloud of smoke.

I CAME OUT for my first curtain call to the most thunderous applause I'd ever been met with, or ever could have imagined. Palms clapped, feet stomped, voices whooped. I curtsied deeply, smiled until my face hurt, and blinked back tears of happiness, while starry-eyed young men showered the stage with flowers and love sonnets.

After more curtain calls than I could count, I came back onstage with the rest of the cast. Antonio walked out with us, and we all joined hands. Strands of hair had come loose from my careful coiffure and stuck to the back of my neck and the sides of my face. I was drenched with sweat, but so was everyone else. It felt wonderful.

The thunder of applause mounted. I spotted Graziana and Fortunato, standing near the front of the pit. They smiled up at me, and their candid faces shone with the love of true friendship. My eyes darted to the box Paolina and Margarita were sharing. I couldn't make out their facial expressions, but I saw them spring to their feet and clap ecstatically.

In the midst of the cheering throng I caught a glimpse of Chiara. She neither stood nor clapped. But even in the dusky candlelight I could see her ivory cheeks blaze red with helpless rage. She seemed to fade into the crowd as the applause became all the more deafening.

For a fleeting moment my heart ached that Papà and Mamma weren't able to share my triumph. Yet my soul rejoiced that they were together again, and that my good fortune would help free them from their financial worries. I closed my eyes a moment and prayed that someday I might find a way to help Mamma free the love that had so long been buried in her heart.

Then I was struck like lightning by a startling revelation: For most of this past year Antonio had been there for me when my family wasn't. Even when I'd disappointed him he hadn't turned away. I thought about his students at the Pietà, abandoned by their mothers at birth. Yet the music he wrote for them gave them happiness and a sense of purpose. Now he'd done the same for me. He had transformed his sensitivity to my pain into music of astonishing beauty and energy. And I had given voice to that music. I felt the press of his hand, and my heart swelled with joy. I wasn't afraid anymore.

Suddenly the clamor of applause was punctuated by cries of *Bravissima l'Annina del Prete Rosso!*

I leaned close to Antonio. "Did you hear what they called me?"

He didn't answer but clasped my hand all the more firmly and kept smiling.

LATE THAT NIGHT, while Paolina was sleeping, I crept out of bed and pulled *la moretta* from her hiding place in the back of the wardrobe cupboard. I wrapped a shawl around my shoulders, slipped into soft shoes, and tiptoed down the stairs to the Campo Santa Maria Formosa.

Padding across the square, my nightgown whipping around me, I made my way to the Ponte del Paradiso. I paused on the bridge and held *la moretta* at arm's-length over the railing.

"You can't shield me, and you've failed to silence me," I said, my words ringing in the winter wind. "My voice is free, and so am I!"

I opened my fingers and watched *la moretta* plunge into the icy waters of the Rio del Mondo Novo.

EPILOGUE

L'Annina del Prete Rosso

The Red Priest's Annina

I soon got used to being called *l'Annina del Prete Rosso.* Antonio laughed about it. "I think you're more famous now than I am," he said, pretending to make light of it. But I knew he cherished the nickname as much as I did, because it signified something phenomenal that had grown between us—a communion of two unconventional, irrepressible spirits.

L'Annina del Prete Rosso, they called me. They might just as well have called him *il Prete Rosso dell'Annina*, or *il Antonio dell'Annina*, Annina's Antonio. It would mean the same thing. I belonged to him and he to me—but not in any ordinary way, the way people might think. The bond we shared trumped worldly expectations. We were both free.

In the silence of my heart, I knew that bond could never be broken. My voice had found its home, and its freedom, in the rapture of Antonio's music.

Afterward

Over the next decade and a half, Antonio created a variety of compelling female operatic characters for Annina, all of whom were strong-willed, passion-driven, and resistant to injustice and oppression. During that time he came to depend on her more and more to give life to his artistic vision. In a 1737 letter to a patron, he wrote: "It's impossible to perform the opera without Miss Girò because it's impossible to find another prima donna of her caliber." Annina remained Antonio's close friend, artistic collaborator, and most loyal associate until his death.

Historical Characters

Anna (Annina) Girò (c.1710 - c.1750). Born in Mantua, in Northern Italy, where she met Vivaldi between 1718 and 1720, during his time there as court composer for Mantua's Austrian governor, Prince Philip of Hess-Darmstadt. In 1722 she moved to Venice, under the patronage of the Duke of Massa Carrara. She became Vivaldi's exclusive voice student and protégée no later than 1723, and stayed in close collaboration with him for the next eighteen years, until his death.

Antonio Vivaldi (1678 - 1741). Born in Venice, the first of 8 children of the young Giovanni and Camilla Vivaldi. His father taught him music, and at the age of 15 he began studying for the priesthood. He took Holy Orders in 1703, at the age of 25, and was assigned the ministry of teaching music at the *Ospedale della Pietà*, a foundling home for abandoned girls. In 1710 his first major set of violin concertos was published, *L'estro harmonico* (Harmonic Inspiration), which made him famous throughout Europe. Three years later he wrote and produced his first opera, and from then on divided his time between composing, teaching, traveling, and producing opera.

Pietro Girò (1667 - 1737). Annina's father, a wigmaker from France.

Paolina Girò (1690 - ?). Annina's half-sister, from her mother's first marriage, acted as Annina's chaperone after her move to Venice.

The Duke of Massa Carrara (? - ?). His father had been one of Vivaldi's early patrons. Not much is known of him, except that he was Chiara Orlandi's, and then Annina Girò's, patron in Venice. My "villainizing" of him is fictitious, although it was commonplace for noble patrons of the opera to expect sexual favors from their female protégées.

Chiara Orlandi (? - ?). A contralto from Mantua who had her start in Venice in 1717, in Vivaldi's operas, under the patronage of the Duke of Massa Carrara. While there is no direct evidence that she and Annina had a rivalry, the records seem to indicate that she and Vivaldi had a falling-out in 1720. It is also evident from the documents that the Duke of Massa Carrara dropped his patronage of Chiara when he took on Annina as his protégée. It is a complete mystery why she and Annina appeared in four operas together at the San Moisé theater, apparently without Vivaldi's involvement.

Tomaso Albinoni (1671 - 1751). Venetian composer, ran a singing school. Some scholars believe Annina attended his school briefly before studying with Vivaldi.

Margarita Vivaldi (1680 - ?). Antonio's sister, the second child of Giovanni and Camilla Vivaldi. Antonio in fact lived not only with Margarita but with their parents and another unmarried sister at the Ponte del Paradiso until 1730.

Antonio Gaspari (? - ?). A minor opera singer on Venetian stages beginning in 1712, and impresario of the San Moisè Theater for the 1724/25 season. Like Vivaldi, he was under the patronage of Mantua's Austrian governor, Prince Philip of Hess-Darmstadt.

Maria Maddalena Pieri (1683 - 1753). A contralto who specialized in "trouser" (male) roles. Between 1726 and 1735 she sang in Vivaldi's operas in Venice and other cities.

Graziana, Fortunato, Signora Malvolia, Fiametta, Marzia, and **Ernesta** are fictional characters.

Acknowledgements

Grazie mille to the many scholars, historians, librarians, professors, students, colleagues, and friends who contributed to this project. Their advice, assistance, insights, and expertise have been invaluable to me in piecing together and telling this story.

I'm especially grateful to my readers, Annette Gates, Caroline Smith, Ann Carol Kliethermes-Jones, Charlene McSweeny, Bob O'Brien, Tibby Plants, and Rose Theresa, whose patient encouragement and input helped sustain me through multiple drafts. Many thanks also to Lynn, Ted, Annie, Dee, Judy, Tom, and Dwight for their tireless enthusiasm and honest feedback, and to my two most candid critics, Frankie and Mary Catherine Kelly, who have often made me think twice. I'm also indebted to 19th-century American author W. D. Howells for his lively descriptions of life in old-time Venice.

Most of all, I'd like to thank my husband, Frank, who has escorted me on research trips, listened to me read aloud every draft of every scene, and endured countless hours of Vivaldi opera on long car rides. His wisdom, humor, and love have been my constant source of strength and inspiration.

About the Author

Sarah Bruce Kelly was inspired to tell Annina's story when doing research for a Master's thesis on Vivaldi's theatrical career. She holds a Bachelor's degree in English Literature, Master's degrees in Liberal Arts and Music History, and teaches Italian, Latin, and Fine Arts at a local university and private school. She lives with her husband, Frank, on the South Carolina coast.

Coming soon:

La Girò

By Sarah Bruce Kelly

The Complete Story of Anna Girò and Antonio Vivaldi

Anna's twenty-year love relationship could never be consummated—at least not carnally. The man whose love she covets so desperately is inaccessible romantically, yet he shows his love for her in profound and irresistible ways. The inner demons that torment Anna as a result threaten to destroy this very relationship.

Anna first falls under the spell of the fiery and intriguing *Prete Rosso* at a young age, when Vivaldi is resident composer at the court of Mantua, her hometown. Stifled by the problems of her dysfunctional family, Anna has long dreamed of pursuing operatic stardom, and her attraction to the enchanting Venetian maestro soon becomes inseparable from that dream.

She eventually joins him in Venice, but her road to theatrical success is rife with obstacles such as malicious rival singers, disparaging impresarios, and noble patrons who demand sexual favors. Rumors about the nature of her relationship with her beloved mentor, Vivaldi, abound and lead to dire problems yet, ironically, draw them closer together.

But Anna's growing guilt about her secret longing for him, complicated by her inherent fears of rejection and abandonment, threaten to poison their relationship from within. In the end, Anna discovers that their love for each other has grown into something that transcends their personal relationship—and she finds true love when she least expects it.

La Girò

PROLOGUE

St. Stephen's Cathedral, Vienna 1741

The priest looked at Anna helplessly, his eyes filled with pity. She shivered. Despite the glint of first light through lofty windows, the cathedral's chilling grandeur made her blood run cold.

In the eerie glow of foredawn the dragon-like gargoyles, whose sinister glares had greeted her on her arrival, seemed to embody the demons that had tormented her through the night. Now daybreak suffused the vast sanctuary with an awesome luminance and cast a chiaroscuro of light and shadow over the nave's ghostly plethora of statuary, pillared arches, altars, and sepulchers.

Anna gazed past the priest at the panel that loomed over the high altar, depicting the stoning of St. Stephen, the cathedral's patron. Her heart smarted and sagged at the horrendous spectacle then lurched, as a thrilling sound flooded her ears. Some unseen violinist was playing the most beautiful music she'd heard in a long time. Her eyes met the priest's. He smiled and glanced toward a nearby vestibule. As if a magnetic force were drawing her, Anna walked toward the vestibule, trembling with anticipation.

She peered around the entrance and was astonished to see a dark-haired boy, bowing away so earnestly she almost could have believed it was the composer himself playing. She stepped quietly through the archway and listened, mesmerized, until the music of the boy's violin slowly diminished with an exquisitely tender trill. When he finished he lingered silently for a moment with closed eyes, then lowered his instrument and gazed at Anna, his eyes wide with apprehension.

"*Es tut mir leid*," he said in a bright, high-pitched voice. The child was apologizing to her, and her heart went out to him.

His hangdog expression was punctuated by his pathetic homeliness. He was sallow-complected with a long, bulbous nose too large for his gaunt face, and his lower lip drooped unattractively. Thick black eyebrows nearly obscured his dark eyes. Yet in those eyes Anna detected fiery determination.

She struggled to think how to respond. "*Das macht nichts*," she finally said, then thought she'd better add, "*Das—war—sehr gut.*" She realized her faltering German was barely adequate to reassure the boy and tell him how impressed she was by his playing.

"*Danke*," he replied softly.

"I—um—*Ich spreche wenig Deutsch*," she murmured regretfully.

He eyed her curiously. "*Parla italiano*?" he asked, quite comprehensibly, though in a thick German accent.

"Ah, *sì*, it's my native language. So you speak Italian?"

"*Sì*, signora, rather well, I think."

What a relief to have at last encountered someone she could communicate with, even if it was only a young child.

"The Pater doesn't mind that I'm here," he said, his eyes shifting toward the high altar. Then he looked at Anna anxiously. "You won't tell Herr Maestro Reutter, will you?"

She assured him she would not, although she hadn't a clue who Herr Maestro Reutter was.

"I know I shouldn't be here," he continued, with touching sheepishness. Then his dusky eyes brightened and darted upwards, as if to visually embrace the Cathedral's boundless magnificence. "I just can't stay away, though. It feels so safe and comforting here, so filled with the mysteries of life."

And of death, Anna thought but didn't say. She dabbed her eyes with the handkerchief she clutched in her hand.

The boy's beatific expression faded, and his eyes shone with concern. "Are you all right, signora?" he asked.

"Oh, yes, I'm all right. It's just that I was so moved by

your playing. It reminded me of someone very dear to me."

He took a few steps toward her and seemed to flinch with pain as he moved.

"Are you hurt?" she asked, reaching to aid him.

He declined her offer of help and lifted his chin, almost defensively it seemed. "Nothing to make a fuss about. It's only that at the *Cantorei*, the choir school next-door where I live, the maestro gives us more beatings than food," he said, his ugly, drooping lip trembling slightly.

Anna was horrified. "How awful for you! You poor thing." She looked at his emaciated body and nearly forgot her own troubles. She wanted to take the pitiful little fellow into her arms and comfort him, but something about his proud bearing prevented her.

"Well, that's just how it is, I suppose. But a pretty lady like you needn't worry about such things," he said, drawing himself up with manly dignity.

He almost seemed to be flirting with her. She studied his face for a moment as he looked up at her with eyes that exuded a strange combination of innocence, wisdom, and mischievous charm.

Finally, to soften the subject, she said, "I don't suppose you know who wrote that piece you were playing, do you?"

The boy's face lit up, and his homeliness dissipated in

the brilliance of his smile. "Oh yes I do! The composer himself taught it to me."

Anna was speechless for a moment. "Do you mean to say Antonio Vivaldi taught you that piece?"

"*Sì*, signora," he said, beaming proudly.

The tension in Anna's mouth melted into a smile. "And did he teach you to speak Italian as well?"

"*Sì*, signora!" The boy's grin was endearing, and Anna began to feel genuine fondness for him.

"You couldn't have studied with him very long," she said.

"No, signora, it was only a few months," he said, and his euphoric look dimmed to sadness.

She put an encouraging hand on his shoulder. "You must be a very intelligent boy to have learned so quickly."

"*Sì*, signora," he said with a weak smile. "That's what Herr Maestro Vivaldi told me. He said it was because of my ear for music."

"Then you must have an exceptional ear indeed." She squeezed his shoulder, then withdrew her hand. "You know, you're about the age I was when I first met him."

The boy gazed at her. "Are you a friend of Herr Maestro Vivaldi's, from Venice?"

"I was born in Mantua, and many years ago Maestro Vivaldi was court composer there," she said quietly.

"Is that where you met him?" he persisted.

The weight of memories made Anna's knees droop.

She sank onto a marble bench, and the cold stone walls surrounding her became a hazy blur.

More from Sarah Bruce Kelly:

Jazz Girl

Thirteen-year-old Mary was marked from birth by the "sign of the caul," a powerful signifier in African-American culture. The caul indicates rare powers, especially a tendency toward "second sight." Mary's special gift manifests itself in visions of ghosts and spirits and culminates in an uncanny musical ability.

But her remarkable powers set her apart from her Pittsburgh neighbors, and she is shunned and belittled. The worst culprit is Amy, a neighbor and classmate who delights in getting Mary into trouble. Mary's loneliness is compounded by her mother's cruelty and indifference. Her beloved grandfather, and music—particularly the new "jazz," are all that give Mary a sense of purpose and belonging in the world.

When Grandpa dies suddenly, Mary feels lost. Now she must find her own way through the tangled web of difficulties she faces every day, and her music becomes her refuge. Gradually, though, Mary learns that music is more than just an escape from her problems. By losing herself in her extraordinary musical creativity, she grapples with her inner demons and discovers the true power of her special gifts.

Jazz Girl

PROLOGUE
The Sign of the Caul

Atlanta 1910

"This baby girl been born with a veil over her eyes."

That's what the midwife told my mama the day I came into this world. The ghostly thing called the "caul" that covered my newborn face frightened my mama.

"I reckon she be strange, then," Mama said. At least that's what she always told me she said. The caul went away, but the gift it signified never did.

The midwife said the caul meant I came with the gift of second sight and some people might think that's a good thing. But it's burdened me with a lot of troubles. For example I learned at an early age that my mama didn't love me. Truth was she couldn't abide my strangeness. It spooked her, I guess. When ghosts would visit me in the night and I ran to Mama she never tried to comfort me. She tied me to the bed.

And when I got so scared I stuttered Mama would spit in my mouth to make me stop. The stuttering only got worse. So I just stopped trying to talk altogether. This made Mama and just about all my other relations think I was even more peculiar than they had before.

And because I was so quiet and mopy my step-daddy Winn would get great kicks out of tickling me till I almost had a spasm. One night after I screamed and screamed for mercy from the tickling I dreamed he was smothered by sand. Then he died at the construction site where he worked when a truck dumped a load of gravel on him.

That's when I knew the "sign of the caul," my special gift of seeing, was a powerful thing.

www.ingramcontent.com/pod-product-compliance
Lightning Source LLC
Chambersburg PA
CBHW030817310726
48980CB00006B/524/J

* 9 7 8 0 5 7 8 0 2 5 6 6 7 *